Fool Me Thrice

Sandra R. Andersson

Wordbuilder © 2016

This is a work of fiction. Think you recognize anyone you know? Trust me; it is all in your head.

ISBN: 978-91-88385-13-0

ELEVEN
YEARS AGO

Ok, so she was only seventeen, and perhaps it was a bit too early to draw lifelong conclusions, but this was the most perfect moment of her life, so far.

Caitlin leaned closer and felt the smoothness of Josh's tuxedo against her cheek. The music was just right. She was moving slowly on the dance floor in the arms of the love of her life, wearing the most stunning dress she had ever owned, looking the prettiest she had ever done. The gown was spectacular, and she had been completely blown away when her mother had presented it to her, never ever expecting something so special – so expensive - to come out of the wardrobe of their small rented house. Jill, who was going to beauty school after the summer holidays, had done the entire gang's hair. It had taken hours but been totally worth it. Caitlin felt like a princess, no, a queen, and her king, her knight in shining armor, was right here beside her, where he would always be.

Sure, they were young, but she had known Josh since forever, and she had known for almost as long as that, that they were meant to be together. No one else had ever made her so happy, so very complete, as he did.

It would be so easy for someone like her to resign herself to a life much like her mother's, working odd jobs here and there in their small town, never getting ahead, always just getting by. But she and Josh had plans. They were going to community college this fall, and they would work hard and get good grades, and they would save and scrimp. In three or four years they were going to law school, and they would work hard there as well, and they would become lawyers and get really good jobs and work on important cases and make a real difference in the world. And if that meant that they made good money, what would be the harm in that?

Caitlin did not want to be a lawyer for the money, but she would love to be able to help her mother out, get her a nicer place, something more comfortable and adapted to her needs. Just ten more years or so, then things could start to change for them. Ten years of hard work. It would not be a problem, not with Josh by her side. She knew in her heart that he would be by her side for the duration. He was very reliable, and she knew that he loved her just as much as she loved him. That was why she had accepted the ring when he had offered it to her, even though they wouldn't be able to get married for many years to come.

At first, she had wondered if it was some kind of joke. After all, he had chosen April 1 to propose to her, for no particular reason that Caitlin could think of. She had been quite skeptical, at first, but he had convinced her that he was serious, that it was no joke. That he wanted to be engaged to her, all through college. Perhaps even through law school. It would be a long engagement, but that was fine with her. She knew that it was Josh and her, forever. She knew it in her heart.

Suddenly she realized that the music had stopped. The gym wasn't completely quiet, there were so many people here, and they were talking and laughing, and all the girls' pretty prom dresses were rustling, but she and Josh had just kept moving in tune with the music that was no longer playing. That was the way it was with them when they were together. Everything else just faded away, and they were alone in a small bubble of love, just him and her. It felt good in here. She felt good in here, with him.

In fact, she felt great tonight. The stomach bug that had bothered her the last few days had abated, and she felt on top of the world. Like her feet didn't even touch the ground. Was it going to feel this way for the rest of her life? Would their love be able to stand the test of time and all the problems that they would inevitably come across in life? Yes, she was sure of it. Together, there was nothing that they couldn't do.

There was a piercing sound of feedback from the microphone on stage and she jerked around, let go of Josh and covered her ears. The principal had gone up on stage and taken the microphone from the lead singer.

"I'd just like to say a few words," he began, and Caitlin turned back toward Josh. She was about to say something about the principal's light blue tuxedo but stopped herself when she saw the look on her boyfriend's – no her fiancé's – face.

"Josh?" she said and frowned when he grabbed her hard by the arms. "What on earth …?"

"Please," he pleaded and pulled her closer. "Please, Caitlin, just remember one thing, ok? Remember that I love you and that we are going to get married, ok? Remember that!"

Caitlin stared at him. What on earth was going on? On the stage behind her, the principal was droning on about a couple of the guys on the football team who had gotten scholarships and were going to colleges out of state. People were cheering and applauding the jocks who were grinning from ear to ear. Caitlin lifted her hands and clapped slowly, looking from the jocks to her fiancé. Something was going on, but she had no idea what.

Somewhere in the back of her head, she registered the fact that the principal had continued to speak. She heard the words as if they came from a place far away, even though the speakers were just a few feet behind her.

"And I am sure that most of you already know this, but I'd still like to congratulate Josh Stevenson for his very prestigious scholarship to Princeton. I'm sure you are going to do just great, Josh; you are a bright young man."

Another round of applause but Caitlin barely heard it. Her ears were clogged, as if she had water in them. She just stared at Josh's face, at his embarrassed grin when he looked around the room and bowed a little to thank for the applause and the panic in his eyes when he turned back toward her. The meaning of the news had not sunk in yet. She didn't quite realize what had just happened, or how it would affect her life, but she knew that it was bad. That all the pretty pink happy thoughts that she had just a couple of minutes ago were gone, and would perhaps never return.

"Princeton," she whispered.

Josh hung his head. He almost looked ashamed. Well, he ought to be. Not about the fact that he had been accepted at one of the most prestigious schools in the country. No, even Caitlin didn't think that this was a bad thing.

But the fact that he hadn't told her.

Most of you already know this ...

That was what the principal had said. Now, why would he say something like that?

"How long have you known?" she whispered, and he hung his head almost to his chest. The chest where she had just now laid her head, thinking about their happy future. Together. Not with him halfway across the country and her alone back here. She swallowed hard and raised her voice. "How long, Josh?"

He lifted his head and looked at her. She could see how difficult it was for him to meet her eye. Well, that was something, at least. He knew that he had done something wrong. "Since Christmas," he said, and Caitlin's ears popped. Suddenly she heard everything that went on in that decorated gym. The music had started up again. People were dancing, laughing, flirting, having a good time. And in the middle of it all stood Caitlin and felt her heart shatter in a million little pieces. Sharp, jagged pieces that tore her chest into shreds.

"Christmas?" she gasped and looked around her. Where was the nearest exit? She had to get out of here while she still had the use of her legs. She turned and ran, pushing through the dancing couples, jostling someone who spilled punch all over their dress, mumbling sorry, pardon me, excuse me, under her breath but not caring if anyone got trampled. Just get her out of here!

There was the emergency exit, and she threw herself at it, the fluorescent green bar across the gray door gave in to her push and the door flew open to a gust of cold night air and the ear-piercing noise of the alarm system. Caitlin didn't care. She just stumbled in her new high-heeled shoes over to the road, stopped in the middle of the parking lot to take off the torture instruments and then kept going in her stockinged feet.

Just as she came out onto the pavement in front of the school, Josh caught up with her.

"Caitlin, wait!" he said, and there was something pitiful in his voice, but she did not pity him, not in the least.

She whirled around and faced him. "How could you?" she yelled. "How. Could. You?" She wanted to hold on to the rage – it was where her strength lay right now – but the tears were welling up fast, and she didn't know how much longer she would be able to speak.

He reached out for her but didn't actually touch her. Just as well. "I'm sorry," he said, and it was the ugliest words she had ever heard.

She crossed her arms and glared at him. "Sorry about what? That you didn't tell me that you got accepted to a school miles and miles away? That you didn't even tell me that you had applied to a school miles and miles away?" She took a step closer and started to pull off her ring. "Or that you lied and lied and lied, for months and months and led me on and let me think that you loved me, that I meant something to you, when all this time ..." She yanked the ring off her finger and held it up in front of his face. "... you never had the least bit of intention to marry me. This was just an elaborate April fool's joke!" She threw the ring straight at his face. He flinched when it hit him on the cheek, but he didn't shield himself, didn't do anything to protect himself from her fury. The ring fell to the ground between them, but none of them looked at it. Instead, they just stared at each other, she furiously, he pleadingly.

"Please don't be mad, Caitlin," he said, and her eyebrows flew up her forehead so fast that they were almost singed. "This doesn't have to be a bad thing."

"What? Are you insane?" She spread her arms and looked around her. "In what way is this not a bad thing? This is the worst thing. Ever!"

He shook his head. "No, please, just listen to me. Sure, it's not exactly the way we planned it, but if you would just listen to me, I'm sure that we can make a new plan, just as good as the old plan ..."

Caitlin just shook her head. "It seems to me that you have a new plan. To go off to fancy Princeton and ditch the old girlfriend that you've been stringing along for MONTHS with LIES and EMPTY PROMISES!"

He staggered backward. "No, not at all. No, Caitlin, I would never lie to you ..."

"But you just did," she said and leaned forward poking him in the chest. "You just did. For several months, you've been lying to me, every day. Telling me that you love me, that we were going to be together forever, that we were going to go to law school together ..." Her voice broke. "It was all just a lie," she whispered. "And I was a fool to believe you." She turned and walked away, muttering to herself under her breath. "So stupid. How could I have been so stupid?"

The tears were streaming down her face, and she staggered toward the corner of the street where miraculously a city bus appeared just as she collapsed on the bench by the bus stop. She got up and walked over to the door but stopped on the bottom step, looking around her, confused.

"Are you coming, honey?" said the bus driver, a middle-aged woman with pale freckles and a tired smile.

"I'm sorry," said Caitlin and started to back off the bus. "I forgot … I haven't got my purse … I left it inside … I don't have any money …"

"That's fine, honey," said the woman. "It looks like it's been a rough night. Hop on, I won't tell anyone."

"Thank you," whispered Caitlin and stepped on the bus again. When she sat down on a seat in the back, with her shoes in her hand, she felt the chill of the night air for the first time.

And the chill of being completely alone, for the first time in as long as she could remember.

All alone with no one who loved her.

ONE
YEAR AGO

The Seattle offices were in a skyscraper down-town, on the 25th through 27th floor, with what would certainly have been a spectacular view if it hadn't been raining. Josh walked over to the window but couldn't even see down the block. No, no one came to Seattle for the sunshine. Not in February, anyway.

The door behind him opened, and he turned around. A man came toward him with his hand stretched out.

"Mr. Stevenson, welcome to Seattle," he said and smiled like a used-car-salesman.

"Thank you."

"I'm George Franzen, head of arbitration. I'm glad to have you here. I've put together a team of junior partners, some secretaries and a couple of paralegals to help you prepare for this case."

"That's much appreciated," Josh said. "I'm going to need all the help I can get."

Mr. Franzen laughed deep in his belly. "Oh, I'm sure that's not true. From what I hear about the Mirage case, you're more than capable to take on a case of this caliber."

Josh smiled. Perhaps he had done a good job on the Mirage case, but only as second chair. This was the first time he headed up the entire prep work for a major arbitration. If he messed up, it was going to cost their client millions. And that did not look good on a résumé.

"Thank you, sir," he said and hoped that it didn't show how worried he was. Three years as a lawyer and he still felt wet behind the ears when he went up against men twice his age with ten or even twenty times more experience.

"Come on. I've told everyone to gather in the conference room."

Mr. Franzen led him along a wide corridor and into a large conference room on the corner of the building with windows in two directions. There were about eight or ten people in there, of all ages, about the same number men and women. Josh shook hands and tried to catch everyone's name, even though he knew that he would have forgotten them all by the time he had greeted everyone.

One woman had stayed seated at the table, and he reached past a man who might have been called Tom to shake her hand. She was slow to lift her hand from the table where it had been holding a pen, making notes on a small yellow legal pad. Neat notes, in a small neat handwriting. Just like ...

He lifted his eyes to her face at the same time as he grabbed her hand to shake it. It was ice cold and clammy. Her eyes were wide open and intensely green, and her face was pale, as if she had seen a ghost. It looked incredibly familiar and strangely alien at the same time. The eyes that he had stared into for hours at end were now edged with beginning crow's feet, and there were thin lines across the forehead and around the mouth. The mouth that he had kissed a million times. It was the same mouth, but the lips looked a little narrower and a lot more serious than he was used to seeing it.

"Caitlin ..." he said and tried to swallow, but his mouth had suddenly gone completely dry.

She yanked her hand from his grip and looked around to see if anyone had noticed the pleading tone of his voice.

"Oh, do you two already know each other," said Mr. Franzen and stepped up beside them. "What a coincidence!"

Caitlin looked shell shocked from Josh to Mr. Franzen and back again. "Yes. What a coincidence," she said faintly.

Mr. Franzen turned around and started to outline the work that lay ahead for the team. Josh didn't hear a word he said. It took every ounce of determination he had to tear his eyes from her. He hadn't seen her in almost ten years. Ten long, agonizing years. Ten excruciating years of not knowing where she had gone or what had happened to her.

The last time he saw her had been on the sidewalk outside their high school, a long long time ago in a completely different world.

When Caitlin didn't come back to school after prom, her friends had told everyone that she had mononucleosis. Several weeks had gone by without a word, and it had been the longest weeks of his life, but he hadn't wanted to bother her when she was ill. He had planned, meticulously, exactly what he was going to say to her when she came back to school, how he was going to apologize, how he was going to explain to her what his thoughts had been when he applied to a school far away, and applied for early admission as well. It was never about leaving her behind; that had never been his plan. No, he had wanted her to go with him. It would have been great, the two of them together at one of the best schools in the world. Caitlin would have thrived there. She was so much smarter than him anyway. He just knew that she also would have gotten in if she had applied. In hindsight, it had been naïve of him. It had been sensational that they had awarded a scholarship to a student like him. Lightning would never have struck their small high school twice.

The first work session with the team lasted about two hours. Josh would later not be able to remember a single thing that had happened in those two hours. He had been so preoccupied with her, the way she looked, the way she moved, the way her hand moved across the pad when she took notes. Did she work here, at the Seattle office? As a junior partner? That was amazing!

Eventually, they took a break for lunch. When everyone got up, and the room was filled with the noise of scraping chairs and conversation snippets, he leaned forward over the table toward her. "So, you did become a lawyer, after all. I knew that you could do it."

She just stared at him. There was something in her eyes that he couldn't decipher. Was it anger? Was she still angry with him? But it had been ten years. Surely she must have forgotten all about him long ago. "No," she said sharply. "I'm a paralegal."

When Caitlin saw him there, coming in through the door, her heart stopped. Not literally, of course, but it definitely felt like her last moment had arrived. All the blood left her face, and she felt her palms go all sticky. This couldn't be happening. This mustn't be happening.

She had been doing so well lately. Everything had seemed to work out so smoothly for her during the last couple of years, finally. She had almost stopped being afraid. Stopped being afraid of running into Josh, of accidentally meeting him on the street somewhere. She lived in a completely different part of the country, and in a completely different world. Successful young lawyers didn't shop at Walmart in a small town in Washington State, after all.

But she had ventured out of her small-town, small-time, existence when she started going to night school. First getting her high school diploma, which hadn't been very hard considering she had only dropped out a few weeks early. And then taking that course for paralegals. It wasn't the same as what she had dreamed of, all those years ago, but it was doable. She was never going to law school, she knew that, but paralegal was almost as good. Lawyers needed paralegals, and she would still be able to help people, just not directly.

When her professor from night school had offered to write her a recommendation for one of the most prestigious law firms in the country with offices in Washington D.C., Austin and in nearby Seattle, Caitlin had been a bit intimidated at first. But he had insisted that she could do it, that she was very good at this, and she had believed him. And she had gotten the job. It had been a huge step for her, going to work full-time after so many years of temping here and there and picking up hours at the local supermarket, stacking shelves late at night or on weekends. She didn't make much money as a paralegal, and a large chunk of her pay raise had gone towards upgrading her car to a more reliable model and her wardrobe to something that worked in flash offices like these, but Caitlin had been certain that it had been the right decision to take this job.

Now she was convinced that it had been the mistake of a lifetime.

After only a couple of months at her new job, she was not in a position of telling her boss who she did or didn't want to work with. And being a part of this huge case was a chance to make a name for herself here at the firm. Not just being that new girl, whatshername.

He came over to greet her, and Caitlin stared helplessly at him. To her dismay, he didn't even recognize her at first. How could he not recognize her? She had known it was him the moment he walked in the door, and he could stare her straight in the face and not see her?

Well, she wasn't seventeen anymore. But neither was he. And it had been a very long time since they last saw each other. But still. He had obviously not spent any time thinking about her, wondering what had happened to her, what she was doing, if she was happy. Not like she had obsessed over him, all these years.

Somehow she managed to shake his hand, and saw the realization dawn on him, slowly. Yeah, that's right. It's me. Your old sins come back to haunt you, she thought, but she didn't say it out loud. After all, he didn't look at all haunted, but she felt like she had not only seen a ghost, but the ghost had walked straight up to her and shaken her hand.

Creepy.

The briefing of the work ahead took a while but even though Caitlin tried to focus and take notes, she hadn't heard a word the boss had said when everyone got up from the table. Hopefully, she would be able to catch up, later, He couldn't be here all the time, surely? This was just a brief visit, to put together a team.

They went out to lunch, and Caitlin made sure to stay hidden in the crowd of the other paralegals.

"What a hunk, huh?" said Patricia and raised her eyebrows in Josh's direction. "How are we going to get any work done during the next six months?"

Caitlin felt her stomach flip. "Six months?"

"Well," said Patricia. "At worst. But these things take time, sometimes."

"But surely he won't be here all the time?" Caitlin tried to sound indifferent.

"No," said Susan. "We will be doing the grunt work, and he will swoop in at the end and get all the credit. He'll be going back to Washington soon; I'll bet."

"Washington?" said Caitlin and glanced at Josh. Washington was good. Washington was far. And then they need never run into each other again.

"Well, I heard that he was here for the duration," said Robert and leaned closer. It was obvious that he thought that Josh was a hunk too. "That he got an apartment and everything.

I don't know how much grunt work he's planning on doing, but I think he's planning on sticking around."

Caitlin felt a chill running down her spine. Oh, no. Occasional visits, a day here and there to keep a straight face, that she might have been able to manage, but months on end? Perhaps seeing him every day? Talking to him, even?

They arrived at the restaurant. Caitlin hurried into the ladies' room and locked herself in a stall.

Don't cry, she admonished herself. Don't you dare cry, Caitlin Laura Brannigan.

But of course, she did.

The work was exhausting and heading up a large team of people was a real challenge, but when the verdict came back in the client's favor, Josh felt sure that it had all been worth it. Thankfully the entire process hadn't taken much more than a month, but it had felt like the longest month of his life. He had never worked harder and was looking forward to going back to regular case work, where millions were not at stake at the end of the day.

And he was looking forward to going back home east as well. Not that he had experienced much of what Seattle had to offer, but this was not his home. He liked it in the capital, where he could feel the pulse of the entire country, feel the power surging through the hallways of power and be a small cog in that machinery. Arbitration for large sums of money was a completely different kind of law, and perhaps it wasn't for him. Somewhere in the back of his head, he couldn't let go of the thought that he had become a lawyer to help people, not just to make a lot of money. Sure, the money was nice, he wouldn't ever say otherwise. But he couldn't forget the light in Caitlin's eyes when she spoke of the things that she wanted to accomplish, the people whose lives she would change for the better, the power of law and the responsibilities that went with it.

He hadn't seen that light in her eyes lately. In fact, her eyes had been markedly dark and shuttered. After an entire month of working together, she still hadn't warmed up to him, and he had been sorely pressed to get more than a couple of words out of her. She had done an amazing job on the prep, as he knew she would, but every time he tried to speak to her about something that didn't have to do with the case she found an excuse to leave. Eager to not be around him.

He couldn't understand why, though. It had been ten years, and so much water under the bridge that they were not much more than strangers to each other. But at the same time, there was a connection there, deep underneath. He had felt it as soon as he saw her that first day. And if she didn't feel the same way, then why couldn't she speak to him? Why couldn't she just go out to dinner with him and talk about old times, all the shared memories, everything they had meant to each other once?

Sure, he had made her really mad and disappointed. He knew that. It had been hard to miss it. It had been a completely wrong call, to keep his early admission from her. He had regretted it ever since. But surely that couldn't be the reason why she was so stand-offish toward him now?

He got up from his desk that was now almost cleared of the last month's debris and papers. To think there had been a blotter underneath all that, all this time! He was halfway to the door when it opened. Mr. Jorgensen, one of the founding partners of the law firm, walked in.

"On your way out?" he asked.

"I ... no," Josh said and indicated one of the comfortable armchairs in the corner.

Mr. Jorgensen sat down and put one leg over the other. "Fine job on the case, son."

"Thank you." Josh mimicked the leg thing and tried to look like he wasn't wondering why the boss had come to his office instead of just summoning him.

"I've been thinking. Franzen is retiring in a couple of months, and we're going to need a new man heading up arbitration. Are you interested?"

Josh raised his eyebrows. "I ... was not expecting that," he said diplomatically and carefully molded his features into something vaguely positive but not embarrassingly thrilled.

Mr. Jorgensen waved his hand dismissively. "Never mind what you were expecting. What do you think now that I've asked you?"

Josh honestly didn't know. It was a great career move, money wise. But it would mean that the rest of his career would be all about the money. His own and others. Did he want that?

"Can I think about it?" he asked and tried to look undecipherable.

"Sure," Mr. Jorgensen said and stood up. "But don't think too long, all right? We need someone who can think fast." He laughed at his own joke and sauntered out the door.

Josh got up, closed the door behind him and leaned his forehead against the cool wood. This was great. Except that it wasn't. He didn't know what the right thing to do was, and there was no one he could discuss this with. Every one of his mates would tell him to take the job, get the money while it was offered and start stock-piling a personal fortune. His long string of temporary girlfriends as well. More money for him meant more tropical getaways and more jewelry for them.

But what did he want? He wasn't sure.

He had to talk to someone.

And he could see her face in front of him, even though his eyes were closed.

He found her office, or rather the office that she shared with the other paralegals. He didn't know how they had managed to squeeze all those desks into such a small space, but there must have been shoehorns or maybe even magic involved. They were all packing up for the day, shutting down computers, locking desks, getting coats and handbags and it took a while before someone noticed him standing there.

"Mr. Stevenson," Susan exclaimed. Everyone stopped what they were doing and turned toward the door.

"Was there something you needed?" Robert asked. He looked as if he would be happy to assist Josh in any manner he might request.

Josh looked at Caitlin. "I just ... Could I have a word?" he asked and walked back along the corridor a bit so that they wouldn't be overheard.

She came out into the corridor with her coat on and her purse in her hand. She put a scarf around her neck and looked at him only in the corner of her eye. Why couldn't she even look at him?

"Yes?" she said. As if he was a complete stranger and not someone who once had known everything about her. Sure, that had been a long time ago, in a completely different life, but he had known her body and soul, and it felt so weird standing here with her as two strangers.

He couldn't help letting his eyes wander over the once so familiar body, the curve of her breasts that he had explored for hours at end, the waist that he had put his arms around more times than anyone could count. The long legs that she had wrapped around him, hard and insistent. Surely she hadn't forgotten. She had loved him once; he was certain of that.

"I was wondering ..." he began, but paused. She didn't even look at him, just fiddled with the lock on her handbag instead. He stood there silent until she was forced to turn her head and look at him. It looked as if it pained her to do so. "... if you would have dinner with me tonight," he said.

The look in her eyes was of suffering but was soon replaced by ice and distance.

"No," she said curtly. "I'm afraid I can't." She took a couple of steps toward the elevator. "Was that all?"

He shook his head. "A cup of coffee then? At that place across the street? I just want to ..."

What? He could see the question in her eyes, but was grateful that she didn't voice it. He couldn't have answered. When it came to her, he just wanted … Period. So many different things.

"Just a quick cup of coffee," he said and tried to make it sound like no big deal, even though it meant the world to him right at this minute.

She gave him a small nod and walked over toward the elevators. He followed her into the small space and noted that she stood as far away from him as she could get. So it couldn't be complete indifference on her part, then.

Surely not.

They got their coffees and looked around for a table. There was one small table in a corner, a bit more private, but Caitlin walked straight over to the counter by the window and got up on one of the four or five high chairs there. A couple of the others were occupied already. No privacy. Perfect.

He got up on the chair right next to her. Way too close. She had almost managed to forget his scent, but he smelled exactly the same, even though there was a new layer on top, an expensive aftershave or something. She focused on her coffee mug, taking off the lid, stirring the hot brew with the little stick as if it was essential that she did it just right.

"I've been wanting to talk to you," he began, and her heart shattered into a million little pieces. That was what he had been wanting? Just to talk? Oh, he had no idea ...

And that was the point, wasn't it? He had no idea. He didn't know. Because she had chosen not to tell him.

It had been her choice, and she had to live with that. Now and forever. There were no do-overs, no second chances. He had lied to her and broken her heart, and that had changed her life completely and irrevocably. And here she was now. Ten years later. Aching for him, as if she didn't hate his guts. Because she didn't, of course. She never had.

She had loved him, and that love had become petrified, mummified, turned to stone or maybe a pillar of salt and remained between them forever like some huge obstacle that could never be overcome; like a monument to his lie, to his betrayal.

"What about?" she managed to croak. The coffee was too hot and burned her tongue. Good. Maybe that would help her keep her focus.

"About ... you," he said. "I wanted to ask, how you were doing? How you've been? How you ended up at Kendall, Jorgensen and Stern?"

She looked out the window at the people moving past outside. On their way home from work. Professionals, in their expensive clothes and haircuts that cost as much as her car payments. She almost managed to blend in, but in her own eyes it was obvious that she didn't belong here. How had she ended up at Kendall, Jorgensen & Stern? Through a fluke, that's how. But she couldn't tell him that.

The one thing she didn't want was his pity. Did not want to see him sitting there in his expensive suit, several years into his stellar career and feel sorry for her, that she hadn't been able to go to law school and would never become a lawyer.

"You know," she said and waved her hand dismissively. "It was just one of those things."

He looked skeptical. "Just one of those things? You were going to college back home and then law school, the last time I met you. How did you end up on the other side of the country, as a paralegal? And a relatively new one at that, I gather. What have you been doing all these years?"

Perhaps truth was a virtue. Perhaps lies were evil and would damn her to hell for all eternity. But it would have to do, because she was never going to tell him the truth. She couldn't. Not ever. The truth was hers to keep, forever and ever.

Ten years ago he had made her a proper April Fool with his fake proposal. April 1 was still a couple of days away, but perhaps she could get a head start on this year's fibs.

"Not much," she lied. "Living the spoiled life of a corporate wife." Oh, that was good. A husband. If that didn't make him back off, she didn't know what would.

"Really? You got married?" He glanced at her hand.

Thank God she had decided to always wear a ring to have an excuse to ward of suitors. She pulled her hand away before he could tell that it was a cheap bijou and not the diamond the size of Gibraltar that her imaginary corporate big shot hubby surely would have bought her.

"M-hm," she said and took a sip of coffee to avoid his eye.

"When?"

She didn't have time to think of something elaborate. "I met Brad the summer after high school."

"Where?"

"Here in Seattle. I came out here to visit my aunt."

He was silent for a while. "Kids?" he asked, and there was an edge to his voice.

In for a penny, in for a pound. "Two. Nellie and Julia. Total princesses, both of them. Everything must be pink." She blabbed on about her made-up daughters, and their little dog that they made to wear outfits and their ballet recital recently and how adorable they had been in their little pink tutus.

"So, how come you decided to be a paralegal?" he asked.

"Well, the girls are in school now, and I just couldn't stand the thought of rattling around that big house all alone all day, you know? So, this friend of mine, her husband is a partner in the firm, and he got me a job, well, it's not much of a job, but I keep busy, and my husband is happy because I don't have time to go shopping all day."

She laughed, a fake, hollow laugh, and silenced herself with the rest of the coffee. Now they were even. An eye for an eye, a lie for a lie. Except that his lie had destroyed her, and her lie didn't make the least bit of difference to him. She glanced at him. He was staring down at his coffee mug.

"Anyway, I have to get going. If I'm late to pick up the girls from school again, I'll be forced to chair the next bake sale committee."

He looked up when she got down from the chair and threw her mug in a bin. "Ok," he said. "Thank you for ... taking the time."

He did look a bit subdued, even though she couldn't for the life of her think of a reason why.

"Thanks for the coffee. See you."

And if she didn't break into a run on her way to the parking garage, it was only because of an enormous amount of self-restraint.

THIS YEAR

There was a knock on the door that was slightly ajar and Caitlin looked up. "I'll be just a—," she said, expecting it to be Susan coming to get the final version of the document that she was working on. But instead of Susan's pink Chanel inspired suit and big gold necklace, there was a dark gray pinstripe suit in the doorway. Caitlin dropped her pen.

"Mr. Jorgensen?"

Her boss, or rather, her boss's boss, stepped into the office that Caitlin normally shared with three other paralegals, and looked around at the other desks. They were empty. "Where is everybody?"

"Oh, Robert and Brenda are in court, and Patricia is down at city hall, going through the archives for the—"

He silenced her with a raised hand. He was not here to check up on his grunt workers. That was someone else's responsibility. "That's alright. It was you I wanted to speak to."

Caitlin felt her mouth go dry. Uh-oh. Just when she had thought that everything was going so well. The last two cases she had been working on had both been successful, and if she did say so herself, a small part of the success was down to her hard work. What had she missed? What had she done wrong? Oh, please let it be something that could be fixed.

"I've been hearing a lot of good things about you," Mr. Jorgensen said, and Caitlin slowly exhaled. She hadn't even realized that she had been holding her breath.

"Thank you, sir," she mumbled and hoped that her cheeks weren't as red as they felt.

"That Feldman case you were working on; Mr. Constantine tells me that the information that you uncovered was instrumental in getting the company to accept our settlement offer."

Caitlin looked down. Now her face really was glowing, that she could feel. "It was a team effort, sir," she said, but couldn't help smiling a little. It had felt so good, handing over her report to Mr. Constantine and seeing the look in his eye when he realized that she had managed to get a source from the company to admit that they knew about the leaky valves long before the date in the official documents. The settlement that Mr. Feldman had received would not make up for his lost leg, but it more than covered the medical expenses and the cost of making his family home wheelchair accessible. It had felt really good to be a part of that, but Caitlin didn't feel comfortable being praised.

"Now, now," Mr. Jorgensen said. "I think you are selling yourself short there. I spoke to a couple of the other partners, and they all agree that your contribution here at the firm has surpassed what we would have expected of a paralegal, and we all agree that this type of hard work and dedication deserves to be rewarded."

Caitlin didn't know what to say. "Oh, that's not necessary, Mr. Jorgensen. I—"

Mr. Jorgensen stepped closer to her desk and pulled out an envelope from his inside pocket. "Here's a little something that will hopefully convey how much we appreciate you here, Caitlin. Keep up the good work!"

Caitlin took the envelope and hoped that Mr. Jorgensen didn't notice that her hand was trembling. "Thank you, Mr. Jorgensen. I'm just glad to be a part of the team."

"An essential part, Caitlin. Remember that."

She nodded and smiled. "I will. Thank you."

When Mr. Jorgensen had left she untucked the flap on the envelope and pulled out the small piece of paper inside. It was a check. For $10 000! Caitlin leaned back in her chair and just stared at the number. She had never seen that many zeros in one place before.

So much money! What on earth was she going to do with— She didn't even need to think about it. She knew exactly what she was going to spend her surprise bonus on. And who she was going to bring.

Josh was walking back to his office after lunch when he heard someone call out his name. He stopped and turned and scanned the lobby for a familiar face. A woman was coming toward him with her hand stretched out.

"Mr. Stevenson, how lovely to see you. I didn't know that you worked here in Austin."

"Mrs. Selby, what a pleasant surprise! Yes, I do, since a couple of months now. How are things in Seattle?"

"Oh, you know. We keep busy. Did you hear about the Feldman case?"

"I did. That was a good settlement."

"It sure was. We had a great team on it. Many of the same people who worked on your case, actually. Brenda and Robert. And Caitlin, of course. She did a great job."

Josh felt the mention of her name as a punch in the gut and had to struggle to keep a straight face. "That's great to hear. How is everyone?"

"Oh, fine, just fine. Brenda got engaged. And Caitlin apparently got a big bonus. Well deserved, I must say. Such a hard worker. And what a waste of a great mind. She would have made a wonderful lawyer."

"Yes," said Josh with a pang. She would have. But being a wife and mother was also very worthwhile.

"I do think that it is a shame that law school is predominantly for the well-off," Mrs. Shelby continued. "I do believe that we as a profession would benefit from having people with more diverse backgrounds, and not just in peripheral functions as paralegals and such, but as lawyers in the front row, don't you think?"

"Er ... yes, of course," Josh frowned. Diverse backgrounds? What was she talking about? "But it is of course ultimately her choice ..."

"But that's exactly my point; it isn't. Someone like Caitlin, no matter how sharp her mind is, no matter how suitable she would be for this profession, that door is just closed to her. And I think that it is wrong. There, I said it." She grabbed his arm and smiled. "Never mind. It's a bit of a pet peeve of mine. I think it is such a waste of talented young people, to make our most prestigious educations only accessible to those with the money to pay through the nose."

Josh smiled. "You won't hear any argument from me. I couldn't have gone to Princeton if I hadn't received a scholarship."

Mrs. Selby grabbed his arm again. "Exactly. But that was never an option for her, after dropping out of high school and becoming a mother."

The image of Caitlin with a newborn child at her breast flashed before his eyes and Josh almost flinched. "Well, now that the children are older, I'm sure she could manage law school, if that is what she really wants. It is a lot of work, after all," he said and swallowed to try and shift the lump in his throat. "Perhaps she would rather spend that time with her family."

"Sure," said Mrs. Selby and nodded emphatically. "But even if she had wanted to, she couldn't ever have chosen a different path. Law school is forever out of her reach. She could never afford it. And that's exactly my point. It is such a waste."

"I'm sure her husband—"

Mrs. Selby interrupted him. "Oh, there's no husband, dear. Didn't you know? Caitlin is all alone with that poor boy. Has been from the start."

Josh stared at her. "Boy? I thought she said that she had two daughters?"

Mrs. Selby shook her head. "No, that's Susan, the junior partner. I'm talking about Caitlin. The paralegal. You know, the pretty blonde?"

Oh, he knew exactly who she was talking about, alright. But at the same time, he had no idea what she was saying. "Oh, right. Caitlin. I think I know who you mean. So, she's a single mother?" He tried to make it sound like a casual question, nothing important, just making con-versation, but he could hear his heartbeat pounding in his eardrums.

"Yes, has been from the start, as I said. Such a sad story! Apparently, the boy's father was her high-school sweetheart, and he was killed in a car accident. So sad. On the night of their prom, can you believe it? It's like something out of a movie."

A movie? More like a nightmare. Josh didn't know how he managed to finish the conversation, but a few minutes later he found himself sitting at his desk, staring at his switched off computer screen with his mind racing.

He heard snippets of their short conversation being played back, over and over in his head. "The boy's father" "Her high school sweetheart" "Killed in a car accident". What was this? What was going on? Why had she lied to him, such blatant lies, made up a husband and two daughters? He was certain that he hadn't gotten her mixed up with Susan or anyone else. How could he have? Every word she had said to him during the few minutes they had spent together had been permanently etched into his brain. Two daughters. That's what she had told him. Pink tutus. Corporate wife.

Had it all been a lie? He reached for the intercom and pressed the button for his secretary.

"Laura? Something has come up, and I have to go out of town for a few days. Could you please cancel everything on my calendar this afternoon and get me on the next flight to Seattle?"

There was a moment of pause before he got a reply. "Certainly, Mr. Stevenson."

Caitlin stepped down from the twirling attraction on trembling knees. "Oh, my," she said. "I think I'm going to have to sit down for a while now. How about some ice cream?"

Her son grinned from ear to ear. "Sure. But afterward, we go again, right?"

Caitlin started to shake her head, but then she just smiled at him. "Alright." She couldn't say no to Thomas. He was her entire life, and it was an amazing feeling to finally be able to give him such a spectacular treat. He was a good boy and never asked for things that he knew that they couldn't afford, but she knew that he had dreamed of going to Disneyworld for many years. And here they were.

It had been a wonderful day, and they had both enjoyed the rides and the spectacular sights, but as they were sitting down on a park bench with their ice cream cones, Caitlin couldn't help but notice that her son was stealing glances at the other park guests. It was mostly families. What Caitlin couldn't help but think of as "real" families. Mommies and daddies and their children. Of course, not everyone lived their lives like that; she knew that. But it seemed that everywhere she turned, there was a man and a woman smiling affectionately at each other at their children's excitement over meeting Goofy or getting their picture taken with one of the Disney princesses. Selective awareness, she told herself. It didn't mean that the world was entirely made up of nuclear families. It just meant that she had noticed that her son was particularly interested in the daddies that they saw. And perhaps also that she was feeling a bit lonely.

Lonely, yes. It had been a struggle, raising her son all alone, or with the help of her mother and aunt, and she had been so busy and worked so hard that she hadn't had time to feel the solitude. But her son was older now, and not constantly clinging to her and sitting in her lap anymore, and there was a certain emptiness beside her. And inside her.

If she thought about it, she wouldn't want to live her entire life alone, of course not. She wanted to love and be loved, perhaps even have more children if she could do it with someone. But the reality of getting from where she was to where she wanted to be was just too overwhelming. She couldn't imagine meeting someone, getting to know them, letting them into her life, and her son's life. What if it didn't work out? What if she got hurt again? What if her son got hurt?

No, it was better this way. Just the two of them. They were doing fine.

When they came back to the motel, late that night, after having watched the fireworks and seen all the lights transform the amusement park, Thomas was tired but revved up.

"Mom, can I go in the pool? Can I?"

Caitlin was exhausted, but at the same time she knew her son, and she knew that he would never be able to go to sleep with all that adren-alin and excitement pumping around in his skinny body. "Ok, go get changed," she said with a sigh and went into the bathroom to get a towel.

The motel was not overly fancy, but the pool was big and reasonably clean. After checking in last night, they had been the only guests who used it for a late dip before tucking in, but tonight there was someone else splashing in the turquoise water.

"Daddy, Daddy, look at me! I'm swimming!" shouted a small girl who was paddling around with pink puffs on her upper arms.

The man sitting on the sun lounger by the side of the pool smiled wearily at his daughter. "I can see that, honey. Great job."

Caitlin felt her son grabbing her arm, shy all of a sudden. She nodded to the man and sat down a couple of sun loungers away from him. "Go on, honey. Get in the pool. It's getting late."

Thomas reluctantly let go of her hand and walked very self-consciously over to the side of the pool. He glanced at the small girl and her father and then dove in. He hit the surface of the water perfectly and hardly made a splash.

"Did you see that, Daddy?" the girl exclaimed. "Did you see what that boy did? Did you?"

The man nodded. "I saw, honey. Very impressive." He smiled apologetically at Caitlin. "I think someone had a little too much fun at Disneyworld today. It's going to take a while to get her to wind down."

Caitlin nodded. "Yeah, I know what you mean. We've been there all day, too. I don't know how they do it. I'm exhausted!"

The man laughed. "Precisely!"

He looked at his daughter again, and Caitlin couldn't help but study him in the corner of her eye. He didn't look tired. He looked great. Tanned and smiling and fit and ...

Uh-oh. Caitlin turned toward her son and tried to focus on him instead. That way trouble lay, she thought. But she couldn't help noticing that her son was also casting long glances at the daddy by the side of the pool, and felt a stab when she saw the longing in his eyes when the man lifted his daughter out of the water and wrapped her in a large towel.

That poor boy.

Growing up without a father wasn't easy, she knew that firsthand. That emptiness inside couldn't be filled with other things. God knows that she had tried, and many others before her. Perhaps it had been selfish of her, to keep all others at arm's length all these years. Think what a difference it could have made in her son's life, if he had grown up with a man like that as a step dad.

She watched the man dry off his daughter with the towel and help her put her bathrobe on. "Time for bed, sweetie," he said and pulled her wet and tangled hair away from her pretty face. "A quick shower, a short story and then bed," he corrected himself.

The daughter wasn't going to be told. "A loooong bath, with bubbles. Two stories. And then bed," she said and stuck her little button nose up in the air.

Caitlin couldn't help but smile. "Sounds like you have a long night of negotiations ahead of you." The words just slipped out, and she almost wished that she hadn't said anything.

But then the man turned toward her and smiled. And what a smile. It twinkled and shone and radiated such intense joy that she was completely stunned. "Yeah, she's going to be a lawyer, this one."

"Oh," said Caitlin. "Like her dad?"

The man laughed. "Er, no. Not quite. I'm a plumber. But this one has got some brains on her. She's going to do great things one day."

The girl protested. "I'm not going to be a liar, Daddy. It's bad to tell lies. I'm going to be a princess."

The man raised his eyebrows. "Well ... ok. If you work hard and get good grades, you can be anything you want to be, sweetheart." He winked at Caitlin, who wanted to say something witty, but suddenly there was a large lump in her throat, and she didn't think that she could get a word out.

Work hard, get good grades and don't get knocked up by some lying, deceitful boy. Then you can be anything you want to be. Otherwise, you have to settle for paralegal.

Her eyes stung with tears, and she hurried to grab the towel that was lying on the sun lounger beside her. "Thomas. Time to get up."

She walked over to the pool, holding out the towel.

"I'm Fred, by the way," the man said. "And this is Jennifer."

"Princess Jennifer!" proclaimed the little girl.

Caitlin couldn't help but smile, even though it felt as if her heart was breaking all over again. "I'm Caitlin," she said. And then she curtsied deep and bowed to the little girl in her father's arms. "Your majesty." The girl giggled.

Thomas came out of the pool and Caitlin wrapped the towel around him. "It was nice meeting you," she said and started walking back toward their room.

"You too," Fred said.

"Me too!" said Jennifer.

When Thomas had fallen asleep, Caitlin sat on the couch in the small living room/kitchenette, channel surfing without seeing what was actually on any of the channels that she surfed past. A million thoughts were going through her head. Or perhaps just one. The thought that Fred might come knocking on her door, with a baby monitor in his hand. Asking if she would like to have a beer, talk a little. Get to know each other. Discover shared interests and slowly fall in love.

Or just tear each other's clothes off and have sex until she passed out from pleasure.

She groaned quietly and changed the channel again. It had been so very long. Way too long. She knew that. But somewhere along the line, she had managed to build such a massive wall between herself and her emotions that she didn't even know where to begin to let some man into her life. That Fred guy was of course way too good to be true, and he was probably making mad passionate love to his wife at this very moment, but some other man.

Someone who wasn't Josh. Who wasn't like Josh. Who wouldn't hurt her as Josh had done.

But when she fell asleep on the couch, it was with an image of Josh on the inside of her eyelids.

He couldn't wait until next day's direct flight and had to settle for a six-and-a-half-hour flight with a stop-over in Phoenix. Plenty of time to think. And he had plenty to think about.

Caitlin had a son. A son that might be his. Was probably his. Was almost definitely his.

The thought was mind-boggling, but it did explain a lot of things. If Caitlin had been pregnant at the prom, that would explain her violent reaction and the fact that she had left town without saying goodbye. If she had a child that was his, that would explain why she had told him all those lies about her husband and their daughters, pretending that she was happy to be a paralegal, not regretting her choice to not go to law school.

It would explain why she had not gone to law school. That thought stopped him cold. All of a sudden he saw her life — as a single mom, without an education, getting by on minimum wage jobs, making do, struggling — projected on top of his own life — law school, bar exam, lots of hard work, definitely, but that hard work had its rewards, both monetary and otherwise. The dichotomy of their existences made his head split in two. Part of him wanted to confront her and make her tell him the truth, the whole truth and nothing but the truth. But another part wanted to apologize. Make amends for his part in the reckless stupidity that had cost her the dream of one day being a lawyer.

On the connecting flight that left Phoenix, Arizona a little after 8 PM, another thought plagued him. What would have happened if she had told him? If she had phoned him up after the prom and told him that she was pregnant. That they were going to have a baby. What would he have done then?

His first instinct was that he would have done the right thing. That he would have stayed behind and helped her raise their child. As a couple, if she would have ever forgiven him for not telling her about that stupid early admission thing. Or just as co-parents.

But what would that have meant? If he had gone to community college, just as they had planned, instead of Princeton? Would he be where he was now? He wanted to think that he could have gotten into Princeton Law on the basis of his good grades from their local college, but knew deep down that it was unlikely. Or any really good law school, for that matter. And if he hadn't gone to an ivy league school, he certainly would never have landed a job interview at Kendall, Jorgensen & Selby.

The truth was that he wouldn't have the life he had now, if she had told him. But what life would he have had? Had he been stuck working a small practice in their hometown, struggling to make ends meet, handling divorces and helping people make out their wills? He tried to picture himself in a small, dingy office, taking any client who walked in the door to keep the books in black and hating every minute of it. He couldn't do it. And a part of him knew that he might have made another choice, even if he had known.

Perhaps he would have left her, even if he had known. And did that make him a monster? After all, she had left him. Taken his child and hidden it away forever. She had been selfish, and perhaps he would have been too.

But the question was, what was he going to do now? Now that he knew? Now that the choices had been made, and they lived their very different lives in different parts of the country? When he had his education and his career was well under way.

What was he going to do about this child?

He tried to picture it, but it was impossible. He just couldn't. It was one thing imagining Caitlin with a small baby in her arms, but it was more than ten years ago now. That child would not be a shapeless little bundle in her arms. It would be a person, an individual with opinions and expectations of his own.

The boy thought that his father was dead. The realization hit him like a steel-toed kick in the stomach. It was almost too much. Things like this didn't happen. Not outside of daytime soap operas. He rubbed his forehead and pressed his eyes closed. The thought of having grown up without his own father, not having his reassuring presence, his dependability, his wisdom to fall back on, it made him sick. What would his life have been like if he hadn't had his dad's love and support along the way?

The plane landed a few minutes after 11 PM, and he wanted to rush straight over but forced himself to check into the airport hotel and get some sleep. After several hours of tossing and turning, he got up, took a shower, got dressed and went to collect his rental car. He hadn't had any difficulty in finding Caitlin's address in the Kendall, Jorgensen & Selby personnel files and the rental car's GPS took him straight out of the city and along winding coastal roads to a small town, tucked away between the foot of a mountain and the intensely blue-gray sea. He pulled up outside a small house on a stamp sized lot, with a small lawn in front and a carport on one side. The paint was a bit faded, but the property had a well-kept and cozy feel. There were flowers in pots on the porch and a small bike leaning against the side of the carport. A small blue bike. On the front of the carport was a basketball hoop. Josh swallowed and got out of the car. This was it. He was going to meet his son for the first time. He stole a glance in the side mirror but didn't see anything apart from the panicked look in his eyes.

He walked up to the front door and pressed the doorbell. He heard it chiming inside of the house and listened for footsteps. But instead of a child's bounding footsteps, he heard slow, dragging steps approaching the door. It opened slowly, and an older woman peered out at him. At a second glance, he realized that she perhaps wasn't as old as he had first thought, but she was leaning heavily on a walker, and her face was lined with pain and fatigue. She stared at him as if he was death coming to collect her.

"Josh," she gasped, and as soon as he heard her voice he recognized Caitlin's mother. She had been ailing already when he and Caitlin were in high school, and it was obvious that her condition hadn't improved over time.

"Mrs. Brannigan," he said. "It's good to see you. Could I please speak to Caitlin? I'm sorry to call so early, but it's imperative that I speak to her before she goes to work."

The woman shook her head. "She's not here, I'm afraid. She has gone away for a few days. She won't be back until Monday."

"Monday?" Josh felt the panic grip him. There was no way he could wait that long. "Where is she? I've come all the way from Austin, Texas, and it is imperative that I speak to her, Mrs. Brannigan. Today."

"I'm sorry that you've come all this way for nothing, Josh," the woman said. "But I'm afraid that she has gone to Los Angeles over Easter. As I said, she'll be back on Monday. I'll tell her you stopped by."

Josh ground his teeth. "Where is she staying in Los Angeles? Where can I find her?"

The woman walked over to a small table underneath a mirror. A couple of brochures were lying in a bowl, and she opened one of them and wrote something down on a post-it note. She returned to the front door with the bright yellow piece of paper between two fingers. "This is the number of the motel where th— she is staying. Perhaps you can reach her there. Otherwise, you'll have to wait until Monday."

Never. He couldn't wait another day for this conversation. He thanked Mrs. Brannigan and rushed back to the airport.

When Caitlin and Thomas came out from their room the next morning, ready for another day at Disneyworld, the first thing they saw was Fred and Jennifer come out of a room a little further along the building.

"Good morning," Fred said, and Caitlin blushed when she remembered her thoughts from the night before.

"Good morning," she replied.

Jennifer was wearing Mickey Mouse ears, and her excitement was infectious. "I'm going to Disneyworld," she said. "Again!"

"Me too," said Thomas, a little less shy than the night before. He was also pretty excited.

Fred and Jennifer got in their car, and Caitlin and Thomas started walking toward the shuttle bus stop. "Have a nice day," Caitlin said when they walked past.

Fred shook his head. "Why would you take the shuttle? You can come with us. You'll get there in half the time.

"Oh, no, we couldn't," protested Caitlin but Fred wouldn't take no for an answer.

The drive was a lot faster than the meandering shuttle, and since they were so early, they found a good space, not that far from the entrance. Once inside, there didn't seem to be a reason to go their separate ways. The kids were getting along, and the conversation flowed comfortably, once Caitlin had gotten over her initial embarrassment. They moved from attraction to attraction, had lunch together and after that it was no longer a question of not spending the entire day together.

Caitlin had thought that the day before had been one of the best of her son's life, but she could easily see that this day was something completely different. Having a small friend to ride the attractions with, walking between his mother and Jennifer's father, Caitlin could see the change in her son. He glanced at Fred, mimicked his gestures and tried to act older and more mature. Oh, how that boy needed a father figure. The realization cut her like a knife, and she started to see Fred in a different light.

That there was no Mrs. Fred had been revealed on the car ride over to the amusement park. Jennifer had explained that her mother lived in New York now, with her wife, and that it was just her and Daddy, except for the summer vacation.

At dinner, Caitlin got up from the table to go and get more ketchup and saw a woman over at the counter glancing appreciatively at Fred. When she noticed Caitlin looking at her, she shrugged and smiled. "You can't blame me, surely," she said. "There's just nothing sexier than a man who is a good father. Your husband is so good with them; it makes my uterus ache."

Caitlin turned and looked back at the table, where Thomas and Jennifer were sharing a basket of fries while Fred and Thomas discussed which attraction should be the next stop. They really did look like a family. All of a sudden she could see a future that she had never even dared to imagine. A life with a man, someone who could be a father to Thomas, perhaps even more children. Doing things together, sharing the burden and the joy of parenthood with a partner. It made her uterus ache a bit too.

Images flashed before her eyes of being pregnant again, of Fred putting his large hands on her round stomach and speaking to the baby inside. She grabbed the counter to steady herself. This was getting out of control. If she was ready to allow a man to get close to her again, that was fine. But she couldn't throw herself at the first eligible bachelor that came along. That is not how love works.

But she enjoyed the fantasy, and she really enjoyed the second day she and Thomas spent at the most magical place on earth much more than the first.

When they came back to the motel, it was dark and both children had fallen asleep. Caitlin opened the door to the backseat and reached in to wake her son, but Fred stopped her.

"Don't. I can carry him, if you can manage Jennifer."

Caitlin looked at him through the dark interior of the vehicle. "Are you sure? He is very heavy."

Fred grinned and walked around the car. "Allow me to demonstrate my manly muscle strength," he said and flexed an arm that wasn't exactly bulging with muscles but looked as if it could endure quite a lot.

Caitlin giggled and walked around to get Jennifer out of her car seat. The girl weighed next to nothing compared to Thomas's solid form, as if her bones were hollow like a bird's. Her pink dress was slippery, and Caitlin had to adjust her grip. The girl smelled of popcorn and oranges for some reason.

They carried the children over to Caitlin's room, and she unlocked the door. Fred carried Thomas inside and raised his eyebrows. Caitlin pointed toward the bedroom and Fred carried the boy inside and put him down on one of the beds. He took off his shoes and put them on the floor and ruffled the boy's hair before straightening his back. They walked back out into the other room, and Fred groaned quietly. "So that's what boys are like, huh? Massive! He doesn't look it, but he weighs a ton."

"I told you so," Caitlin giggled.

He took Jennifer from Caitlin's arms and walked toward the door but hesitated on the doorstep. "Or, we could stay," he suggested casually. "I could put her in the other bed in there. That sofa pulls out, you know."

Caitlin held her breath. He said it so matter-of-factly, as if that was an option. As if it were that simple. And perhaps it was. To some people. But not to her. She released her breath and shook her head slowly. "Don't think that I'm not tempted," she said. "Because I am. I'm just not ready to …"

Fred nodded. "Thomas told me about his dad. But life goes on, you know. I hope you don't plan on grieving him forever. Because you deserve more than that. You both do."

Caitlin felt the sting inside her eyes. Perhaps they did. But she was not ready to take that step. Not quite yet. "Good night."

"Good night," Fred said. And then he left.

Josh had been waiting in his car outside the motel all afternoon, a couple of doors down from Caitlin's room. It was dark before they came back. He didn't know if they were coming by car or bus, and was a bit stunned when a car pulled up right next to him and Caitlin stepped out. A man had been driving, and when they both picked a sleeping child from the backseat of the car and started carrying them toward her room, Josh almost left. But he just couldn't. Instead, he watched Caitlin unlocking the door to her room and letting that man carry the boy — his son! — into the room.

Caitlin's mother hadn't mentioned another man, and neither had Mrs. Selby, but that didn't mean that there wasn't one. The thought of his Caitlin in that man's arms made his blood boil, but he realized that he was being ridiculous. It was more than ten years ago. She wasn't his Caitlin anymore.

But she was his son's mother, and for that reason, he stayed. When the door to the room opened again, and that man appeared, now with the small girl in his arms, Josh released a breath he didn't know he had been holding and rubbed his hand over his face. The relief he felt that the man didn't stay was palpable. He waited until the man had disappeared into the room right in front of his car, before getting out and walking over to her door.

He knocked lightly, so as not to wake the boy, and waited impatiently.

The door opened. "I told you—," she said and then she saw who it was and froze.

Josh shook his head slowly. "No," he said. "No. You never told me, Caitlin."

She had gone completely pale at the sight of him, and part of him thought that it was not more than right, but the other part of him, the bigger and better part, put his hand on her arm and led her back into the room. He sat her down on the sofa and went and closed the door to the bedroom. It was dark in there, and he was grateful for that. He didn't want to see the boy, not yet. He couldn't let that child, his son, distract him from the conversation that they had to have.

He sat down on the other end of the sofa. She was staring straight ahead, not looking at him. "How did you find out?" she whispered.

"Mrs. Selby," he said. "I bumped into her at our offices in Austin."

"Texas?" she said. "Do you work there now?"

He nodded, but she didn't see it. She was still staring straight ahead.

"Why didn't you tell me, Caitlin?"

She didn't reply.

"Don't you think that I deserved to know?"

She shook her head slowly. "I could say the exact same thing," she said, and there was something rough about her voice. Like unsanded wood. It could give you splinters. "Why didn't you tell me? Didn't I deserve to know?" she whispered, and the pain was obvious.

Still, he thought, but then he thought about what his lie had meant to her. How his decision to take a long shot had changed his life — at her expense. And she had a small boy who must have reminded her of that moment, every day of his life.

"I was just a kid," he tried, and she turned toward him slowly.

"Yeah," she said and let the word drag out. "Me too."

They sat like that for a long while, just getting used to being in the same room together and in the same room as the truth. After a while, he started to speak. He explained his reasoning behind the decision to apply to a school that was way out of his league. How he hadn't wanted to jinx it. And how he hadn't been able to tell her, when he realized what it would mean to them.

"I still think that we could have made a go of it," he said. "I would have come home on holidays and ..."

She gave him a look that shut him up.

"Well, at least, I thought that before I knew ..." He turned and looked at the door to the bedroom.

"Don't even ..." she said, and there was an edge to her voice that cut him like glass. "Don't even speak about him. Don't even think about him. You have no right ..."

He sat up. "Actually, Caitlin. I do have—"

"Oh, don't even try," she interrupted. "Don't even try to pull that lawyer crap on me. You absolute bastard. You wouldn't even be a lawyer if it weren't for me. What was it that you wanted to be again? A baseball pro? Or maybe a carpenter?" She raised her hand and pointed at her chest. "I was the one ... I was the one who dreamed of that life. I was the one who was going to change the world. And you ..." She turned away again. "And you ..." She didn't finish the sentence.

He sat silent for a while. It was true. The only reason he had ever considered law was because of what she had made it out to be. "It's true," he said slowly. "I wouldn't be a lawyer if it hadn't been for you. You changed my life. You made me dare to dream bigger. And for that I'm grateful."

She snorted derisively. "And in return, you destroyed me."

"No, Caitlin. That's not—"

"You crushed me," she continued. "You broke me so bad that I'll never be whole again," she whispered. "And I'm not going to let you back in my life so that you can do it again. Or worse, so that you can do it to him." She pointed at the door. "Do us both a favor and leave. I don't want you here."

He didn't move. "That's not going to happen, Caitlin," he said after a while. "I want to meet him. I have to—"

"No, you don't! You don't 'have to' anything. Except leave. That little boy in there thinks that his father is dead. That's what I've told him all his life. If you show up and start telling him otherwise, it is going to destroy him. He won't ever trust me again. Have you any idea what something like that can do to a child? Do you?"

He stared at her. "I can imagine," he said. "But I can also imagine what it must be like to grow up without a father. And if I had known …"

"If you had known, then what? What would you have done if I had told you? Would you have given up your place at Princeton? Stayed in town? Gotten a job at Walmart? Gone to night school to become a paralegal? Like I did? Would you?"

He was quiet for a while. "The truth is that I don't know. I don't know what I would have chosen. But I didn't get a choice. You now have a choice. You can choose to keep me away or to let me be a part of that boy's life. I've missed so much, Caitlin. It feels terrible. But I would like to be here for the rest. If you'd let me."

She shook her head. "I could never tell him that I lied. He would never forgive me."

"You don't have to. You don't have to tell him that I am his father. Couldn't I just be an old friend? Or a new one?"

She looked skeptical. "I don't … I don't date much. He is not used to having men around."

"How do you think that he would react? Would he mind, if there was a man in your life?"

Caitlin looked down, and he could see that the question bothered her.

He pointed at the plastic bag from Disneyworld that was lying on the coffee table. "Is that where you were today? Did he love it? Would you like to go again tomorrow? I'd like to take you."

She glanced at the bedroom door. "No, thanks. We've been there two days straight. Tomorrow is our last day here, and I'd like to do something different. Something less frantic."

"Can I come?"

She looked like she wanted to say no. "I don't know what we are going to do."

"That's ok. Can I take you both out somewhere? Will you let me?"

"We were going to go to Los Angeles and just hang out. We've never been."

He smiled. "Well, I have. Will you let me be your guide? I can come and pick you up tomorrow morning at nine, and we'll have a day out in LA. How does that sound?"

Judging by the look on her face, Caitlin would have rather had a root canal, but despite that she nodded slowly. "Promise you won't say anything to him?"

He crossed his heart. "I promise."

She grabbed his arm and stared straight into his eyes. "Don't. Hurt. Him. Whatever you do …"

"No. Of course not."

Reluctantly, Josh got up and left. When she closed the door behind him, he couldn't help but wonder if she would be here when he showed up at nine. Better make it seven thirty, he thought. Just to be on the safe side.

Caitlin hadn't been able to go to sleep after Josh had left. Instead, she had showered, packed and prepared everything for the morning, so that they could just have breakfast and leave. Exhausted, she more or less passed out on the other twin bed sometime after three and thought that there must be something wrong with the alarm when it went off only a few seconds later. But no, it was 7 AM already, and she needed to get going. She wanted to be out of here by 8 to be on the safe side.

But Thomas was not in the mood for an early morning. The two days at Disneyworld had taken its toll, and he wanted to sleep in. Caitlin went in to wake him several times, but at 7.30, he was still asleep. Cursing under her breath, she went out to the small kitchenette and fixed herself a cup of instant coffee. Just as she was stirring to dissolve the cryo-beans, there was a light knock on the door. Caitlin froze, but when there was another knock she hurried to get the door. Whoever it was, she didn't want them to wake Thomas.

Josh was standing outside the door. He looked like he had slept as bad as she, but he smiled when he held up a tray of takeout mugs and a bag that smelled divine. "Good morning, sunshine."

She stared at him. "You said 9 AM."

He stepped inside and looked pointedly at the bags that stood right by the door. "And I guess you were hoping to be out of here by 8?"

She could feel her cheeks betray her but closed the door and followed him over to the small table by the kitchenette.

"I didn't know what you like so I got a couple of options for you. And a hot chocolate for ..." He turned and looked over at the bedroom door. Then he turned back and stared at her. "I don't even know his name."

"Thomas," she said. "After my grandfather."

He nodded slowly. "Tom?"

She shook her head. "No. Never Tom. Always Thomas."

"Ok." He looked at the door again. "Is he up?"

"Not yet."

He pulled out a chair and sat down. "Ok. Have a baked good while we wait."

She sat down across from him. The cappuccino he had brought smelled much better than her cremated instant and when he tore open the paper bag it was filled with all kinds of baked breakfast pastries. "You sure know how to treat a lady," she murmured under her breath.

He smiled and took one of the other mugs. "You used to think so."

She blushed and took a curler. The pastry was still warm and perfectly flaky. "Please don't say stuff like that in front of—"

The door to the bedroom opened before she had time to finish the sentence and a skinny boy emerged, rubbing his eyes. "What is that smell?" he said and then stopped and stared at the stranger sitting at the table.

"Good morning, Thomas," Josh said. "I'm Josh. An old friend of your mother's. I brought you two some breakfast. Would you like something to eat? I've got you some hot chocolate."

Thomas stared at him and then at his mother. Caitlin didn't know what to say, but she tried to smile. Josh continued. "Your mom told me that you were going to LA today, so I came by to drive you. Saves you schlepping all those bags on buses and trains."

Thomas approached the table slowly, taking in the offered pastries, his mother and the stranger. "If you are an old friend, how come I've never met you before?"

Caitlin went cold, but Josh looked calm when he replied. "That's because I knew your mother before you were born. We went to school together."

Thomas's eyes narrowed. He sank down on the chair next to his mother and regarded the stranger with a frown. "Did you know my dad as well, then? 'Cause he went to school with my mom."

Josh swallowed and tried to sound calm when he replied. "Yes, he said. I knew him well."

Caitlin raised a hand to cover her mouth and looked like she was going to cry.

Thomas stared at him but didn't say anything more. Instead, he took a pastry and nibbled it slowly. The crisis seemed to be averted. For now.

The drive to Los Angeles took a little more than half an hour. When they were getting closer, Caitlin picked up a brochure from her purse. "There's a museum that I thought might be interesting. It's on—"

Josh glanced at Thomas in the backseat. He was looking out the window and hadn't said a word the whole time. "Is that what you would like to do, buddy?" he said. "Go to a museum."

Thomas pulled a face but didn't say anything.

Josh smiled. His mom had been just like Caitlin. Always trying to make every trip "a learning experience". "I was thinking that we could go down to Venice Beach. Check out the street performers. See the ocean. How does that sound?"

Thomas shrugged, but Josh thought that it looked as if he was making an effort to look indifferent.

Caitlin turned and looked at her son. "I don't know ..."

Josh reached out and put his hand on her arm. "Trust me. I've been to Los Angeles many times. I know where to go, what to do. You will have a good time. Both of you."

Caitlin put the brochure away and didn't say anything. Not until they came closer and she started to notice the buildings and the signs and the people moving about.

Josh parked the car, and they went for a walk along the boardwalk. It was like a mad cross between a circus, a freak show and a country fair. The sun was shining, and the weather was nice, even if it was a bit too cold for the beach. They got ice cream and made their way through the crowds until they found a place to sit with a view of the ocean.

"Pretty neat, huh?" Josh said and elbowed Thomas lightly.

Thomas didn't reply at first. Instead, he looked at Josh with that frown again. "Could you tell me something about my dad? Did you know him well?"

Josh glanced at Caitlin, who looked panicked. "Yes, I knew him pretty well," he said. "Since we were kids."

"Mom says that he was very brave," Thomas said, almost accusingly. "Was he, really?"

Josh leaned back and looked at the boy. At certain angles, the boy was uncannily like himself at that age. "Brave? In what way?"

"Mom says he was the only one who dared to jump from the high cliff, where they used to go swimming."

Josh smiled. That was one of his proudest accomplishments, but bravery? No. "It's true that he jumped from the cliff."

"Were you there? Did you see it?"

"I was there." Josh looked at the boy. He looked almost disappointed to have his mother's story confirmed. An iconic father like that might be a difficult role model to live up to for a small boy. "But I can let you in on a little secret. It was nothing to do with bravery."

Thomas looked confused. "How do you mean?"

Josh leaned closer and spoke in almost a whisper. "He didn't jump because he was particularly brave. He jumped because he wanted to impress a girl."

Thomas's eyes widened. "What girl?"

Josh glanced at Caitlin. "Who do you think?"

Thomas turned and stared at his mother. "You never told me that."

Caitlin looked from her son to his father. "I didn't know." She looked at Josh. "Is it true?"

Josh nodded. "Your mother and her friends were always hanging out on the small beach next to that cliff. There's nothing scarier than a whole gang of girls, am I right?" Thomas smiled and nodded. "I— Your father told me that he wanted to ask your mother out, but he could never get her alone long enough to get her attention. He came up with the ridiculous and completely reckless plan to jump from the high cliff when your mother and her friends were watching. If it didn't kill him, it would be sure to get her attention."

Thomas turned toward his mother. "Did it work?"

Caitlin smiled a bit embarrassed. "It sure did. He got my attention, asked me out, and that was it. It was him and me from that day on." She ruffled her son's hair with a sad smile. "But if I ever hear of you doing something stupid like that for some girl ..."

"Oh, yuck!" said Thomas.

Josh laughed.

After the beach, they went out on the Santa Monica Pier. When she saw the lights, crowds and attractions, Caitlin balked and protested. That was not at all the nice and quiet day that she had planned. But Josh steered them away from the carnival and the noise and crowds and down into the Aquarium under the Pier where they wandered around, amazed at all the wondrous creatures. At 3.30, they watched the sharks feed and after that, they walked back up in the pier to feed their own growling stomachs. Josh took them to an Italian restaurant, with a rooftop bar with a view of the Ferris wheel where Thomas devoured a pizza with the same fervor as the sharks had attacked their dinner. Caitlin picked at her eggplant parmesan while

Josh mostly ignored his ricotta and spinach ravioli and instead looked at Caitlin and Thomas.

After the initial skepticism, Thomas had overcome his shyness and kept asking Josh questions about his father and the small town where they had grown up. Josh replied as truthfully as possible and eventually got over the strange feeling of speaking about himself in the third person. He could tell that the boy latched on to every piece of information, cherishing every morsel he was given, every piece of the puzzle that was his dead father.

But of course, he wasn't dead. He was sitting opposite him in the restaurant and telling him one of his own childhood memories, about his parents, that of course was Thomas's grandparents even though he might never even meet them. It was a fishing story, and Josh could tell that Caitlin was thinking the same as him, that if she had told Josh about the pregnancy, Thomas would have gone fishing with his father and grandfather.

Caitlin kept glancing at the time, and eventually she interrupted their conversation. "I'm sorry to break up the party, but we really need to get to the airport if we're going to catch our flight.

Josh could see the disappointment on Thomas's face, and if he were completely honest, he felt pretty disappointed too. He hadn't gotten a chance to speak with Caitlin alone all day, and he hated to see her go before they had discussed the future.

"Why don't you stay an extra night?" he said. "Fly back in the morning?"

Caitlin shook her head. "That's not possible, I'm afraid. The tickets are non-transferable. It's now or never."

Never, thought Josh. Please, let it be never. If they got on that plane now and he flew back to Texas, then what? Nothing had been decided, nothing had been resolved. They needed to speak. Needed to get over the past and plan for the future.

"I'll get you new plane tickets for tomorrow," he said and hoped that it didn't sound too desperate. "Stay just one more night. How about if I call the place where I usually stay and ask them if they have two rooms available? It won't cost you a penny, I promise."

Caitlin looked like she wanted to decline, like she'd rather be on her way to the airport right now, but he could tell by the way she looked at her son that she was torn.

"Please, mom," said Thomas. "Can we? Just until tomorrow?"

Just until tomorrow. Just a few more hours. Caitlin smiled and put her hand on her son's cheek. Her smile looked strained, but the affection in her eyes was genuine.

"You really want to? Ok. We can stay one more day." She turned toward Josh. "But I insist on paying for our room."

Josh leaned back and reached for his phone to make the call. "I'll make sure they make out a separate bill for you," he said and smiled.

The drive was pretty long, and the roads were winding here and there so that Caitlin was completely lost long before they got to where they were going. When she realized that they were driving through a residential neighborhood, she sat up. This was not what she had expected. She had pictured a fancy executive hotel downtown or perhaps something near the airport, but instead, they were driving past Spanish-inspired villas and carefully manicured gardens.

"Where are we going?" she asked quietly.

Josh kept his eyes on the road. "It's not far."

"That was not what I asked."

He didn't reply. A couple of minutes later, he turned into a wide driveway and parked the car in a double carport.

Caitlin looked around. "Where are we?" she whispered and glanced over her shoulder at Thomas, who was unbuckling his seatbelt. "Who lives here?"

Josh switched off the engine and got out of the car. "You'll see."

Caitlin hurried out of the car but didn't follow him over to the front door that opened before he had rung the bell. A middle-aged woman in a flowery dress stepped outside and held out her arms.

"Mrs. Stevenson," she whispered and looked around for an escape route. There wasn't one. They were stuck here. This was inevitable.

"Where are we?" said Thomas and got his bag out of the trunk.

"Well, that is his mother," said Caitlin and hoped that the panic she felt didn't leach out into her voice. "So I guess that this is his parents' house. They must have moved." She walked over to the front door with her son by her side.

"Caitlin, dear, it's so good to see you again," the woman said.

"Mrs. Stevenson, it's nice to see you too," Caitlin replied.

"Oh, please," said the woman." Call me Jordan. And who is this young man?" She reached out her hand and Thomas shook it.

"This is Thomas," said Josh. "Caitlin's son. They've been at Disneyworld for a couple of days, and I talked them into staying one more night so that we could catch up. I told them that they could stay here."

"Well, of course they can," Jordan said and stepped to the side to let them in. "I've made up the beds in the guest room. Come on in. Have you eaten?"

"Yes, thank you," said Thomas and looked around him in the spacious hallway.

"Josh, why don't you show Caitlin where the guest room is, and I'll get some milk and cookies for young master Thomas here. You do eat cookies, right? You're not allergic or anything?"

Thomas shook his head and grinned.

"I'll just put our bags away, sweetie," Caitlin said. "We'll be right out."

But Thomas had already followed Jordan out into the kitchen and didn't look particularly worried about being left alone in a strange house.

Caitlin followed Josh through to the back of the house into a small but cozy guest room overlooking the back garden. As soon as the door had closed behind them, she grabbed his arm and turned him toward her.

"Are you insane? You can't ..."

But Josh looked completely calm. "Can't what? Can't let an old friend who is in from out of town stay over at my parents' house for just one night? So that we get a chance to catch up and have a proper conversation out of reach for small ears — a conversation that we really need to have before you go back."

Caitlin crossed her arms. "You should have told me where we were going."

"You would never have come." He put his hand on her arm. "Look, I realize that this is hard on you. But it is seriously difficult for me as well. You've known all this time, and I just found out the day before yesterday. I'm trying to make the best of a very complicated situation, while making sure that Thomas doesn't get hurt. My mom doesn't know, and I won't tell her if you don't want me too. But think about it. Your son is having milk and cookies with his grandmother in the kitchen right now. For the first time in his life. Doesn't that feel kind of … good?"

She wanted to protest, but instead just shook her head. "I have to go out there. I need to hear what they are talking about."

"It's going to be fine, Caitlin," he said, but he said it to her back. Caitlin was already out the door.

Thomas and his grandmother were sitting in a glazed-in garden room off the kitchen, talking about Disneyworld and Venice Beach and all the other things that Thomas had seen during the last few days. Caitlin sat down and just listened to their conversation. Jordan didn't say much, but Caitlin knew that Josh's mother was a clever woman, and since her son was the spitting image of his father at that age, she didn't expect to be able to keep her secret much longer. She felt the weight of the world on her weary shoulders, trying to keep everything together during this long and intense day after just a few hours' sleep and in the proximity of a man that made her feel all too much. So many regrets, such intense memories and such heart-breaking pain and grief that it made her clench her fists until her nails made small half-moon shaped indents in the palms of her hands.

It was late and only took about a half hour or so before Thomas began to yawn. "Time for bed, I think," Caitlin said and had to restrain herself to not run for the door.

Jordan got up. "My husband won't be home until late, I'm afraid. But I know that he will want to meet you in the morning. What time do you leave?"

Caitlin glanced at Josh. "I'm not sure. We changed our flight. I don't know exactly what time the new tickets were for."

Josh got up. "There will be time for break-fast. But I'm pretty beat, so I think I'll turn in as well." He kissed his mother on the cheek and followed Thomas and Caitlin into the house. When they came out into the hallway, he stopped by the stairs.

"My room is the first one on the right, upstairs," he said under his breath so that Thomas wouldn't hear him where he stood looking at a wall of family portraits and holiday photos. "Why don't you come upstairs when he has fallen asleep? Then we can talk."

Caitlin didn't reply. She just shook her head. Going up to his bedroom? Well, that was never going to happen. She knew that they needed to talk, but did it have to be today? She was just too tired and wouldn't be able to think straight or make any decisions. "Come on, sport," she said and put her hand on Thomas's shoulder.

Thomas ignored her and pointed to one of the framed photographs. "Who is that?"

Josh walked over and looked at the photo. "That's me, at summer camp."

Thomas looked disappointed. "Oh."

"Come on," Caitlin said again. "Time for bed."

When Thomas was tucked in and on his way to fall asleep Caitlin heard him mumble something from the other bed where she sat, staring out the window at the darkness outside.

"What was that, sweetie?"

"For a moment, I thought it might have been my dad, in that picture."

Caitlin felt her mouth go completely dry. "Why would you think that?"

Thomas turned over and fluffed his pillow. "Because he looked just like me when he squinted his eyes against the sun like that," he said, closed his eyes and fell asleep.

Caitlin sat there and stared at her son with tears in her eyes. She wished that she could just tell him the truth, that Josh was his father, that Jordan was his grandmother. It was so obvious from the way he had interacted with both of them that he really wished that he could have had a dad like that. Sure, he had his Grandma back home in Seattle, and Auntie Meg too, but Caitlin's mother had been sick for many years and had never been able to run around and keep up with her active and energetic grandson. Having a second set of grandparents would mean a lot to him. And she knew that Josh had two sisters and a brother. Perhaps Thomas had cousins? He would definitely love that.

But if she told him all that, she would also have to admit that she had been lying to him his entire life. And that she had kept all these wonderful people from him.

Caitlin sighed and wiped her tears. Thomas would never forgive her for that. He would get an entirely new family, a father, grandparents, aunts and an uncle, lots of cousins.

And she would lose her only child.

His room here in Los Angeles was nothing like his room back home, thankfully. It would have felt weird to end his first day as a father by going back to his old room where he had slept as a child. This was more of a permanently assigned guest room. There were some of his old books in the bookcase and some framed photos on the walls, but not a shrine to his childhood, that he knew some parents kept. Thank goodness for that.

He sat down on the bed and looked out the window on the darkness outside. There were almost too many emotions to be able to tell them apart. But he thought that he was mostly happy. Sure, there was some bitterness about the things he had missed out on, all the opportunities lost. But mostly, what he felt when he looked at Caitlin and Thomas was joy. Excitement about the next phase of his life. The parent phase.

He had never really thought about having children, besides being very careful when it came to birth control. But that wasn't because he didn't want to have any children. Just that he hadn't yet met someone that he had wanted to start a family with. There hadn't been anyone that he had felt as deeply about as he had with Caitlin. Despite the unsatisfactory way that their relationship had ended, he had always felt a connection to her. And now it turned out that there had always been one. A child.

He didn't know how, but he knew that he wanted to be a part of his son's life. Not just pay child support and have visitation rights. He wanted to be there, at the breakfast table, taking him to school, picking him up after practice, tucking him in at night. He wanted to be a proper dad, just like his own father had been.

He just hoped that Caitlin would let him. He would have to tread gently during this conversation. She was worried about letting him back into her life, he could tell. All of this was happening so very sudden, so completely unexpected. Unexpected for him because he hadn't had any idea. And unexpected for her because she had known all along.

He sat down in the armchair over by the window and took out his phone, checking his email and the news. He couldn't remember the last time he had gone all day without getting in touch with his secretary. Laura must think that he had been abducted by aliens.

He shut the phone down, put it on the table next to the bed and just stared out the window. How much longer before Caitlin showed up? Was she going to show up? She hadn't seemed very eager to have this conversation now. In fact, she had seemed like she just wanted to get out of here, go home and lick her wounds. She had looked a bit shell-shocked, to say the least. It had been an intense day.

Perhaps it had been unfair of him to spring his parents on Caitlin like that, completely out of the blue. But he had felt at a disadvantage and it was good to have some backup. He picked up his phone again and scrolled through his contacts. Then he called one of them.

"It's me," he said when she answered. "I'm in town for the night. Why don't you come over for breakfast? Bring the whole gang! The more, the merrier."

Caitlin waited until the entire house was quiet, before sneaking out to the kitchen for a glass of water. She had been crying so hard that she felt completely wrung out and needed to replenish her fluids before she fell asleep. If she was ever going to fall asleep in this house. It didn't feel very likely.

The house was dark, but there was enough light coming from the digital displays on the appliances that she could find a glass and fill it from the dispenser in the door of the large side-by-side refrigerator. The water was so cold it hurt her teeth and tasted very clean. She took small sips and stared at her own reflection against the darkness outside the kitchen window. What a day this had been. She was so very glad that it was over.

"I was beginning to think that you weren't going to come," a voice said just to her right. Caitlin jumped and spilled some water over her hand.

"You scared me," she whispered and wiped her hand on her pajama bottoms.

He came into the kitchen. "Sorry. I thought you heard me coming down the stairs."

She shook her head.

He studied her face. "Have you been crying?"

She turned away and started to wash the glass.

"Just leave that in the sink," he said, but she rinsed off the detergent and found a towel to dry it with. When she was done, she put it back in the cupboard where she had found it.

"You forgot to wipe down all surfaces for prints," Josh said and winked at her. "A professional CSI-team will still be able to prove that you were in this house.

She turned toward him. "Don't worry. I wore gloves," she mumbled.

He laughed quietly. "Are you done? Shall we go upstairs?"

Caitlin looked at him, pleadingly. "Can we please do this some other time? I ... I really don't feel like I can do this now. It's not that I'm trying to be difficult, but I don't think I can handle this conversation. Not tonight."

He walked closer and put one hand on her arm. "I know that this is hard for you. Trust me; it's no picnic for me either. But we have a lot of decisions to make."

"But do we have to make them tonight?" It felt as if she would start to cry again and she didn't want to do that in front of him.

He grabbed her by the other arm and pulled her closer. "Please, don't be sad." He held her gently and slowly stroked her back with one hand. "I don't want to make you upset. I want to try and think of this as a good thing. That I found out."

He let go and led her into the dark and empty living room where they sat down on one of the sofas. "It's so easy to focus on all the things that I've missed out on. The entire pregnancy, the birth, the first ten years of his life.

So many firsts. So many important milestones. In his life and in yours. But I can never go back and do any of those things. I can't change the past. It is what it is. But the future. From this moment forward, I can change things. And I don't want to miss any more milestones. I don't want my son to go one more day without a father. Or at least, a father figure."

Caitlin stared at him. He sounded so sincere. But had he really thought this through? What it would entail? "But ... How did you plan to change all that?" The thought made her completely exhausted.

He leaned back against the sofa cushions. "I don't know. But it's all doable."

"Is it, though? Is it, really? You live in Texas; we live in Washington State. I don't even know if you are married or have a girlfriend or something. You have your career; I have mine. And Thomas is not used to having a man around the house. I don't know how I would explain that this old friend of mine suddenly shows up and wants to spend lots of time with him."

Josh stared at her. "Married? I'm not married. Never have been? How about you?"

Caitlin shook her head. "No, never."

"Alright then. That settles it. There is one easy solution that fixes all your reservations in one go."

"What?"

"Marry me."

A nervous laughter escaped from her lips, and she slapped one hand over her mouth to stop the sound. It echoed through the silent house, and she listened to hear if anyone had woken up. The house stayed quiet. Everyone slept. "Please. Be serious."

"I was. Completely serious. I can't think of a single reason why not."

Caitlin crossed her arms. "I can't marry you. I don't even know you. You don't know a thing about me. And I certainly don't trust you. So there's a few reasons why not, at least."

"What do you mean, you don't know me? You know all there is to know about me. You know me better than anyone."

"If that's true, then it's very sad. I haven't seen you in more than ten years. Sure, we were very close, once. But we were just kids. We've grown up since then. At least, I have. I had to."

He frowned. "I have too. But trust me, I'm still that guy. A few years older, a few pounds heavier. But deep inside, where it counts, I'm still the same person you fell in love with. That you had a baby with."

She rubbed her hand over her face. "If that is true, then you are also the same person that broke my heart in so many pieces that I've not been able to trust a man since then. I could never marry a man who might do that to me again. I could never let my son get close to someone he couldn't trust. Someone who could just leave."

He leaned closer and took her hand. "Oh, Caitlin. If you had any idea how sorry I am for what happened that night. I never meant to hurt you, and I honestly didn't have any idea that you would take it so bad. It was stupid and naïve of me to think that we would be able to work it out, and I should have discussed my plans with you, I really should. But all of that is in the past. And just like the things that I've missed with Thomas, I can't change any of it. I wish I could go back, do things differently, make better and more responsible decisions. I was just a scared and excited kid, and I made mistakes. I kept some things to myself that I ought to have shared with the most important person in my life. And I got my fiancée pregnant. But I meant it when I proposed to you that time. I believed that it was you and me forever. And I believe that it can still be. If you'll just find it in your heart to trust me again."

She wanted to pull her hand away, but there was something about the feeling of his fingers wrapped around hers that just felt so very right. How many times had they sat like this, on a sofa somewhere, in front of a TV, not caring what was on, just having eyes—and hands—for each other?

"Please," she said. "It was an accident. We were careful, just not careful enough."

He stroked the back of her hand with his other hand. "We got a bit carried away, perhaps. I seem to recall that we sometimes did."

She couldn't help but smile. That was putting it mildly. They had been teenagers, after all, and all that curiosity and all those hormones had been a dangerous combination. Lethal. Explosive. "Perhaps a bit."

His hand wandered a little further up along her arm. "It was like that with us, right from the start. It was a good relationship, all the way up to the very last minute."

She nodded. That was true. "But the very last minute more than made up for all of it," she said, and the grief in her voice was palpable.

He squeezed her hand harder. "Did it? I mean, I know that I hurt you, and I wish more than anything that I could go back and do things differently, but did it, really? Did it erase all the good times, all the wonderful memories, all the love? Can't you remember any of that?"

She stared at her hand in his, felt the warmth of his palm against hers. Of course, she could remember it. But the good memories had been intertwined with the pain and humiliation and over the years a thick layer of regret and disappointment had settled over everything like a layer of dust, obscuring and annihilating all that had been good.

"Don't you remember, Caitlin? What it was like, before? During all those years, before? I know I hurt you badly, but that was just one night, one of so many. Don't you remember all those other nights, when I made you feel good? Remember, Caitlin?"

His hand was all the way up on her shoulder now, massaging gently, easing out all the knots and all the tension. She wanted to deny it, wanted to shake her head, but her body didn't want to lie anymore. She nodded. "I remember," she whispered hoarsely.

"Mmm," he said, quietly. "I remember, as well. I remember this," he said and leaned forward, placing his lips ever so gently on hers.

It was exactly the way it had always been, and at the same time completely different, in every way. Apart from their very first kiss, he had never been shy when he approached her, never afraid of being rejected. But now, with all the tension between them, it was like making love on a mine field. With his entire life on the line. But it was worth it, of course. Worth it all.

The pajamas didn't put up too much resistance, and they were soon entwined on the wide sofa, moving, touching, kissing, even crying. He could taste the salt on her cheeks, feel her body trembling with emotions underneath him, and all the grief and sadness over lost time and irreversible mistakes mingled with the pleasures that he rediscovered in her and created a beautiful and powerful tapestry of life at its fullest, love and hate, joy and sadness, hope and disappointment.

Entering her body was like coming home to a place he had been missing for so long that he didn't know if his memories had been warped. Sure, some things were different, those lines on her stomach, the shape and weight of her breasts, but other things were exactly the same. Like the sound of her breathing beside his ear when he pushed inside of her, the way their bodies seemed to move as one, responding, communicating, giving, taking, the way she pressed her nails into his back at the moment of climax, the intense euphoria of release, of letting go and collapsing on top of her, completely spent and utterly happy.

He reached out and found a blanket, folded up on the backrest. He pulled it over them and settled beside her, still with their legs intertwined, still with the taste of her in his mouth.

She was crying, soundlessly, and he kissed her tears away, caressing her cheek.

"It's ok," he whispered. "Everything is going to be ok."

She shook her head. "You don't know that. You can't promise me that."

He put a finger under her chin and made her look him in the eye. "I can promise you that I will do everything in my power to make you and our son happy. Whether or not you marry me, I promise you that."

She looked doubtful. Then she sighed. "I loved you so very much," she said, and the pain in her voice cut him deep. "And you hurt me so very bad."

His hand wandered from her cheek, down her neck, over one breast and down her side. "I'm so very sorry," he said and kissed her again. "I want to make it right." He pulled her closer and hugged her tight. "I want to make you trust me again," he whispered. "I want it to be you and me again, the way it was. Only better."

He kissed her cheek and then continued down the side of her neck, hearing her contented sigh and taking that as an invitation to proceed. But when he settled between her legs again, she stopped him.

"We can't," she said. "I'm not on the pill. We shouldn't have done that."

He lay down beside her again and kept caressing her. "That's ok. There are other things we can do." He kissed her again and then moved down along her body, kissing her breasts, her stomach, all the way down to the place where he ached to be. She put her hand over her mouth to keep from screaming out loud, but he could feel her reaction all through her body and smiled when she grabbed his hair and pulled hard. He kissed her on the inside of her thigh and looked up. "That's right, baby. Just let it go."

She looked down at him with hunger in her eyes. "Are you sure that you don't have a condom somewhere?" she said. "I really need to feel you inside of me."

He moved up and lay between her legs, his hard length pressing against her soft warmness. "Sorry. No. This was not planned. Not at all."

She pouted a little, but gave him a kiss and reached for him. "I guess we'll just have to make do."

He laughed softly. "Oh, you make it sound like such hardship."

"Well, you've got the hard part right," she said and gripped him firmer. He moaned.

"Would it be so bad?" he asked, after a while. "If you got pregnant again? I mean, what is the worst thing that could happen? That we have another baby? Another child, just as amazing as the one sleeping in my parents' guest room?"

She smiled. "He is the best thing that ever happened to me, so if something like that would be the worst thing, then perhaps that wouldn't be so bad. Except ..."

He released her grip on him and moved in between her legs. "Except what?"

She spread her legs and let him in. "Except that I really like my job." She moaned and leaned her head back. "If I had another baby ..."

"I'll stay home and take care of the baby," he said. "I'd love to. But I still don't think that you ought to go back to work."

She looked up. "What do you mean?"

"I mean, I think that you should quit your job," he said. "Because you ought to consider a different career." He moved slowly but determinedly, feeling the pressure build.

"Josh?" she said, and there was an edge to her voice that told him that he'd better stop. It took all of his restraint to do so.

He stopped and raised himself up on his arms. "I think that you should go back to school. Go to law school. Become a lawyer."

She laughed. "I couldn't. Not ever."

He looked down at her. She was the most beautiful person he had ever seen. But she was also the smartest and most determined person he had ever met. "You could, you know. I'll pay for law school. You don't have to marry me, if you don't want to. You don't have to have another baby, if you don't want to. Except, at the rate this is going I think that we are definitely going to get pregnant before this night is over. But what you do have to do, is go back to school. That is the one thing that I will insist on."

She stared up at him, those intensely green eyes that he loved so much, that he had missed so much. This was exactly what had been missing in his life all these years. This closeness, her presence. If she didn't want him in her life, he didn't know what to do. Except that it wasn't just about the two of them anymore. Through their son, they would always be connected. He just hoped for so much more than a shared custody.

"Do you mean it?" she whispered, and he supposed that it was a lot to ask of her to trust him.

He nodded and kissed her on the forehead.

"I mean it. I love you, and I want you to be happy. And whatever else happens between us, I think that you fulfilling your dream is essential."

She kissed him back, cautiously at first but soon more intensely. They resumed their love-making and before long they were clinging together, sweating and laughing. Caitlin rolled around and lay on top of him, looking down. He raised one hand and pushed her hair out of her face.

"What do you say?" he asked and braced himself for her answer.

She sat up, letting the blanket fall to her hips, and he feasted his eyes on her naked shapes. "I don't know what to say. This is all so sudden. I can't believe that you've thought this through. I don't believe that you really want to marry me. It's been too long."

He stared at her. Too long? Yes, it had been. But she had not left his heart in all this time. And he might have a way to make her believe it. He looked around him.

"Where are my pants?"

"Ok," she said and gathered the blanket around her to cover her breasts. "You don't have to rush off like that. I'm just being cautious."

He smiled and rooted through the pockets for his wallet. "Here it is." He opened it and pulled out a small ring. The one she had thrown at him, outside the school gym, that night so very many years ago.

She just stared at it, confused at first and then wide-eyed. "You kept it?"

He lay back down and looked up at her. "Of course I did. You were the love of my life. Even if I had never met you again, I would never have forgotten you, not as long as there was life left in me. April 1 is not until Friday, but I think that is close enough that we can still claim that as our engagement date. So what do you say?"

She looked confused. "What is it with you and April 1? I never understood why you chose that day."

He smiled a little. "It is a very important date. It is the anniversary of the day when I knew that I was in love with you."

She looked even more puzzled. "But we started dating at the end of summer. Like, August or maybe even September."

His smile widened. "Oh, but that was years later. The April 1 I'm talking about was when we were ten or so. Do you remember Bobby Jensen's tenth birthday party?"

She frowned and thought back. "I think so. Was it the one where …?" She quietened.

"Yes. A couple of the other boys tricked me into thinking it was a masquerade party, and I showed up dressed like a dinosaur. A huge green suit. Tail and all. Everyone laughed at me, the entire time, and I was boiling in that padded suit, but I couldn't take it off, because I only had my underwear on underneath."

"You poor thing," she said and put her hand on his cheek. "I remember now. Your cheeks were all red when I sat down next to you. And I thought it was because you thought that I was pretty. When in fact it was just that you were covered in polyester and padding." She laughed.

"I did think that you were pretty," he said. "And I thought that you were so nice, when you didn't laugh or make fun. You just sat down beside me, and we had some cake and talked about school and stuff, and before long I didn't even remember that stupid dinosaur suit. I was just so happy that I had gone to that party, so that I had gotten to spend that time with you. And I knew then that you were the most amazing girl I had ever met, and that I would have to get up the courage to ask you out. It only took me five years or so, but I did it."

She stared at him. "I had no idea. All those years?"

He nodded. "All those years. And all the years to come. You are still the most amazing girl that I have ever met. And I'm not just saying that to get in your pants, because, well, they're all the way over there and you are over here, straddling me, naked."

She blushed but smiled a little at the same time. She shook her head but then her face split up into a blazing smile. "I say: Yes!"

His eyes widened. "Yes? Yes to what?"

She smiled. "Yes to all of it. Yes, I will marry you. Yes, I want to have another baby with you. And yes, I want to go to law school. If you'll help me with my homework."

Another night with not enough sleep, but Caitlin still smiled when Thomas shook her awake the next morning. "Mom? Mom? Are you awake?"

She turned around and looked at her son. "I am now. What's up?"

Thomas was already dressed. "I'm hungry. Can we have some breakfast?"

Caitlin sat up. An enticing smell of pancakes and bacon came from the kitchen. Jordan didn't need to go around the house knocking on doors to get her guests out of bed. "Ok. Let me just put some clothes on."

Walking out into the kitchen with her son, Caitlin couldn't help but blush. She could see the sofa from where she stood. The blanket was folded and lay neatly over the back, but she still thought that it was obvious to the world that something had happened there last night. If they couldn't tell just by looking at her.

Jordan had really gone to town, and the breakfast counter was piled high with pancakes, cereals, bacon and eggs, rolls and bagels and different spreads, cheeses and ham. She smiled at them when they came in through the door. "Good morning. Did you sleep well?"

"Yes, thank you," said Thomas and eyed the pancakes.

"Good morning," Caitlin said and tried to look unruffled. It was difficult.

"Have a seat," Jordan said. "Coffee?"

"Please."

They had breakfast and chatted a little, about Los Angeles and Seattle and why Jordan and Bill had chosen to relocate when Bill retired.

"Well, the weather was a big factor," Jordan said and put another pancake on Thomas's plate. "But mostly it was because Sharon and her family live here. She is the only one of our brood to have kids, and Bill and I wanted to be nearby."

Caitlin felt a lump in her throat and wondered if Jordan suspected anything. "Sharon has kids?"

"Three. Ted is the eldest. About Thomas's age, I should think. Perhaps a little younger. And Phoenix and Madison. They're twins. Three years old now, going on ... I don't know what. They're a bit of a handful. But so much fun. It's never boring, being a grandmother."

As if on cue there was a knock on the door. Before Jordan had time to get up, the door opened, and a cyclone blew in.

"Gramma, Gramma, did you know that cows have four stomachs? Did you? Also, did you know that there is a blue car in your driveway? Did you get a new car? Why do you have two cars? Do you have visitors? Can we have some pancakes? Can we?"

Two small girls stormed into the kitchen, threw themselves on Jordan, constantly babbling. Then they noticed the boy sitting across from her and just stopped and stared. One of them leaned closer to Jordan and whispered theatrically. "Gramma, who is that?"

Jordan pulled out chairs for her granddaughters and gave them each a pancake. "That is Thomas, and you will say hello nicely. Then you will eat your pancakes and once you're done you can go and play in the garden. Gramps put up the new swing for you.

The girls grabbed their pancakes off the plates and ran for the patio door. "The new swing! Yippie!"

And then they were gone. Caitlin just stared at Jordan. Then she turned toward the door to the hallway. A boy was standing there, looking at her. No, looking past her, at Thomas, who was still staring at the patio door where the twins had disappeared. The resemblance wasn't obvious. This boy had blond hair, and he was not as skinny as Thomas. But the shy look was the same. And there was something about the shape of the face and the way he held his head that reminded her so much of her own son. Sharon appeared behind him and put her hand on her son's shoulder.

"Hi, Caitlin," she said and pushed her son ahead of her into the kitchen.

"Sharon. Hello." Caitlin got up to shake her hand, but Sharon ignored her hand and just gave her a hug instead.

"So good to see you again," Sharon said. "It's been ages. How've you been?"

"Fine." Caitlin sat down again. "This is Thomas," she said.

"Hi, Thomas," said Sharon. "This is Ted."

The boys greeted each other with a nod.

"Have you eaten, dear?" Jordan said to Ted. When he nodded, she continued. "Well, have a pancake, anyway. And perhaps you and Thomas could go out back and keep an eye on your sisters, so they don't break something?"

Ted nodded and took a pancake. "You wanna go outside?" he said shyly without looking directly at Thomas.

"Yeah, alright," said Thomas without looking up from his plate. He stood up, thanked Jordan for breakfast and followed Ted out into the garden.

Caitlin followed him with her eyes. Sharon sat down beside her. "Don't worry. They'll soon be playing as if they'd known each other their entire lives. Kids are like that." She took an empty mug from a pile and Jordan poured her some coffee.

Caitlin felt the truth behind the words like salt in her emotional wounds. Sure, kids were like that. But the truth was that Thomas could have known Ted all his life, they could have grown up as cousins and been really close. She took another sip of her coffee and tried to smile.

Sharon asked her what she had been up to, and Caitlin told her and Jordan about her work as a paralegal and a little about life in Seattle. She could hear footsteps coming down the stairs and braced herself. She didn't know how Josh wanted them to do this. So many promises had been made last night, and perhaps the harsh morning light had made him change his mind.

But it wasn't Josh who came in through the door from the hallway. It was his father. "Caitlin, my dear, how nice to see you," he said and came over and gave her a little semi-hug. "I couldn't believe my ears when I came home, and Jordan told me that we had visitors. So great to have you here."

"Thank you, Mr. Stevenson," Caitlin said and almost blushed. He had always been kind and pleasant to her, but she had never received this kind of welcome in their home. It felt uncomfortable, considering she was sitting here under false pretenses and the fact that she had kept their grandchild from them all these years. How would they react when they found out the truth? She couldn't imagine that they wouldn't soon be able to do the math, or just notice the striking similarities. It was inevitable that the truth would come out, but how? And when? And who was going to tell them?

She quickly decided that no one was going to be told until she had told Thomas the truth. In theory, it had been a feasible idea just to let Josh raise Thomas as his stepson, but in reality, this was so much bigger than the two of them. The three of them was just one piece of a much larger puzzle. This was going to affect so many people. She would just have to hope that Thomas would one day be able to forgive her.

Josh could hear voices coming from the garden outside his window. When he looked out, he saw his nieces fighting over a swing hanging from the large tree out back. Then his nephew turned up and mediated and convinced them to take turns. Ted was excellent with his sisters. Any other boy his age with two wild sisters might have just shut the door to his room and never come out again, but Ted was patient and tolerant and could always arrange a peace settlement when the tempestuous twins butted heads.

Another boy appeared in the garden below, and Josh stared at him. His son. He still couldn't believe it. He knew that it was true, of course he did. He had known from the start. The boy looked just like him. But the fact that he was a father, that was a little more difficult to grasp. He had so much catching up to do.

He was looking forward to getting to know his son, and resuming his relationship with Caitlin. The intense emotions were still there, and they had only had to put a match to the kindling to start a roaring fire that he didn't think would ever go out.

It had been ten years. They could have grown apart during that time, grown into completely different adults with nothing in common. But he didn't sense anything different about her, not who she was deep inside. She was still his Caitlin, and he couldn't wait to start his life with her. And their son.

So what was he standing around here for? When his soon-to-be wife and son were down-stairs? He smiled and headed for the door.

The mood in the kitchen when he came down was cautiously cheerful. Everyone was smiling, but he could tell that Caitlin was a bit worried about what he would do, what he was going to say to them. Honestly, he just wanted to walk over to her, give her a big kiss and then tell everyone that Thomas was his son and that Caitlin had agreed to marry him. But he knew that the truth would have to come out in stages. First, they had to tell Thomas. Then his parents. Then the rest.

"Good morning," he said and walked over and gave his mother a kiss on the cheek. "Everyone sleep well?" He turned to Caitlin who looked relieved. "We have about an hour before we have to go to the airport. Would you like to go outside and catch some sun before you return to the cold and rain?"

"It doesn't always rain in Seattle," Caitlin protested, but she did it with a smile. "But I wouldn't mind going outside. The garden looks lovely."

"Go on," said Jordan. "Sharon and Bill will help me clear the table."

It wasn't particularly warm outside, but the sun was shining, and there was no wind here behind the house. The sound of the children laughing made Josh smile. He had always loved being around his sister's kids, their energy and joy was so contagious. But knowing that one of those children over there was his own took those emotions to a completely different level. It was strange to think that one could love a person that one had just met, but that was exactly what Josh felt when he looked at the boy who helped his little cousin re-tie a shoelace. Love.

Then he turned toward the woman standing beside him and felt his heart expand even further. She was also looking at the children, but though she smiled there was sadness in her eyes as well.

"You haven't changed your mind, I hope?" he asked, and it wasn't entirely meant as a joke.

She looked at him and smiled. "No," she said. "Have you?"

He reached out and took her hand, fingering the ring that she had put on inside out, with the stone on the palm-side of her hand. "No," he said. "I meant every word I said last night. I love you and want to marry you. And I will be honored to support you all the way through law school. I'm sure that you will be a great addition to the profession and that you will go on to do great things."

She bit her lip and glanced over at her son. "I'm worried about how he's going to react."

Josh nodded. "I think it will be fine. I wouldn't blame him if he became upset at first. But I'm convinced that he'll get over it. The truth is always best, in the long run."

She squeezed his hand and turned toward the children. "Thomas? Could you come here, please?"

Thomas came running across the lawn. "Yes? What is it, Mom? Are we leaving?"

"Not yet," Caitlin said. "I just wanted to talk to you for a moment."

Thomas glanced impatiently over his shoulder at the other children. "Ok, what is it?"

"Thomas, look at me."

The boy heard the serious tone in his mother's voice and turned toward her. "Yes?"

Caitlin sighed and put her hand on his cheek. "You know the things I told you about your dad? About the car crash?"

He stared at her. "Yes?"

"I'm sorry, baby, but ... that wasn't entirely true."

Thomas pulled away from her hand. "What do you mean? Not true?"

Sharon looked like her heart was being torn into small pieces. A tear rolled down one of her cheeks. "I'm sorry, baby. I thought it was for the best. I just didn't want you to be hurt."

Thomas looked from his mother to Josh and back again. "What are you saying? What do you mean?"

Josh took a step forward. "She is trying to tell you that I am your father, Thomas."

Thomas stared at him. "You?" He glanced over his shoulder at the other children again and over at the house. Inside the large kitchen window, he could see Jordan and Bill at the breakfast counter, laughing at something Sharon had said.

He turned toward his mother. "Is that true? Is he my father?"

Caitlin nodded. "Yes, honey. Josh is your father. He didn't know about you until a couple of days ago. He came looking for us as soon as he found out."

Thomas stared at his father. "So what happens now? Do you go away again?"

Josh shook his head. "No, son. Your mother and I are going to get married. I'm always going to be around, from now on. We're going to be a family. All three of us."

Thomas looked from his father to his mother. "Married?"

Caitlin tried to smile, despite the fear that gripped her. Would her son ever trust her again? Would their relationship be damaged forever? Would she ever be able to regain his trust? "Yes, sweetie. I understand that this is a lot to take in. Everything is going to be very different from now on. But I think that it is for the best, and I am very happy about this. I hope you will be to, eventually. We're going to be a family, just like your father said. But please don't tell any—"

Too late. Thomas was already running across the lawn whooping with joy. "They're getting married! He is my real dad!" He stormed in through the patio door to the kitchen and Josh could hear his voice through the open window.

"You are my grandma and grandpa! This is so cool!"

Everyone got up and came out into the garden where Josh and Caitlin stood holding hands and looking a bit embarrassed. This was definitely not the way they had planned to tell everyone.

But the truth will out, as they say.

In the end.

The End

THANK YOU!

Thank you for reading my little story. If you enjoyed it, please consider leaving a review on Goodreads or Amazon. It helps other readers decide if this is something they would like to read.

If you are curious about my other books you can find out more on my website:

www.saralisaandersson.com

www.ingramcontent.com/pod-product-compliance
Lightning Source LLC
LaVergne TN
LVHW042151190726
843493LV00006B/1613